A DAY LATE

A Michael Christian Mystery

MIKE SAAD

ISBN 978-1-7322499-0-5

Dedication

To my wife Muriel, who has heard the stories repeatedly over the decades and continues to allow me the luxury of boring her while I tell them to first time listeners. For her encouragement of me to take the time to reduce those stories to writing and for her patience with me while I did so.

To My Grandchildren — In 1993, I flew on the Concorde from New York to London in 4 ½ hours. That in itself was an interesting event in my life and I thought it would be fun to tell you about it. But then I figured I should also explain why I flew to Europe. London was only a brief layover on my way to Germany to solve a corporate dilemma my company faced. So, when you read this and then ask the question you always ask about my stories, "Really Grandpa"? The answer is a resounding, "Yes." (Mostly.)

And to my good friends who, over the years, told me "*You really should write a book.*" Well, here you go.

Acknowledgements

Thank you to my continuing friend from childhood, Tom Kowalski, who read all the earliest versions, offering me encouragement, editorial and grammatical comment, and clarification of Russian expressions and idioms.

Many thanks to Shannon Doherty, who agreed to proofread *A Day Late.* And even though she may have underestimated the scope of work, she bravely held forth with great attention to grammatical detail and factual research. I'm very grateful to Terri Kowal who volunteered to read my manuscript and who made excellent grammatical and conversational edits.

Thank you to Lorna Lee of Early Girl Enterprises for her patience in managing my first-time-author anxiety as she prepared the book's final formatting and for her style contributions. To Peter O'Connor at Bespoke Book Covers for his "rocking" cover design.

And to friends Dave and Pat Johnson, voracious readers and book club founders, thanks for reading, correcting and encouraging this work.

Any grammatical errors, mistakes or oversights are all mine and not the result of the fine work of others.

Table of Contents

Preface

ON CHRISTMAS DAY IN 1991 MIKHAIL Gorbachev dissolved the Soviet Union, then promptly resigned. That same day Boris Yeltsin became president of the independent Russian State. This move, while heralded in the free world, created an environment of economic instability that in turn provided an opportunity for the adventurous and the corrupt throughout Eastern Europe.

In 1993, and unbeknown to Michael Christian's Corporate Executives in the U.S., the German Federal authorities had been conducting an extensive investigation. They believed smuggling was going on from within his company's very large manufacturing facility in the city of Reinbeck. When they did not get the expected support for their investigation from plant executives, they closed the plant in an attempt to force the necessary cooperation. It was an extortion of sorts. That got their attention in the States. The next few days proved for Christian to be more than he had bargained for.

This story is based on those events. Many parts of this book are fictionalized, as are all the characters that breathe life into the events. You may think you recognize some of the characters and events in reality. Including Michael Christian, he and all the others are based on conglomerations of personalities and companies encountered over the years, in the worlds of law enforcement and corporate security. The kernel of the story is true. The rest is, as they say, *based* in fact.

Michael Christian and the other characters are completely made up. Any similarity to real persons or companies may be convenient but is merely coincidental.

Chapter One

YEVGENY DIDN'T PARTICULARLY CARE who came and went at the Warnemunde Warehouse. His job was merely to open and close it whenever he was told. If the visitors wanted electricity or lights, he would unlock the circuit panel and provide it. If they wanted water for the toilets he would tell them "no", for the pipes would surely burst in this bitter cold. The owner also wanted him to make sure the rat bait was kept fresh and that the traps were emptied weekly. Yevgeny enjoyed following orders rather than giving them and the job suited him.

When he was called, Yevgeny would unlock the gates and the doors and wait while shipments were loaded or unloaded. The drivers, Anatoly and Gennady, were old friends of his. Every now and then a boat would come also. He would watch the very efficient transfer of a crate or two onto the vessel before it pulled out. The entire process only took minutes. He knew the boat's skipper, Luganov, but since they were not friends, Yevgeny and the old captain never spoke. When the boat was loaded, or his friends finished, he would lock the place back up, say goodbye to his friends and go back to his apartment, alone.

Things had once been better for Yevgeny—during his military years in the Soviet Union. He enjoyed his soldiering days. His corporal's pension had once been decent too. He knew he would never be rich, but he had no such aspirations. He used to have a small walk-up flat just outside Moscow in Khimki, with its own stove and refrigerator. He could clean his clothes in the common laundry room and had fresh groceries when they were available. Although he did not have an automobile he could easily get to the City by bus, which had a stop just down the street from his apartment.

Then Gorbachev dismantled the Soviet Union, ruining everything for him. First his monthly allowance was drastically cut. When his heat allotment went next, he resorted to extra layers of clothing to keep warm. Then he cut back on his beloved Vodka and began eating canned, rather than fresh foods. His pension was only fairly good to begin with but with interest rates rising, he was losing more money each year.

Once the Iron Curtain came down the economy was in a tailspin and he could barely afford to heat his apartment, much less buy warm clothes. *Even that drunk Yeltsin was a better president*, he thought. No matter who was in charge though, things had gone downhill for Yevgeny and he feared his options should he get sick.

Just when things had been most difficult, his friend Pavel called and offered him a job to look after his warehouse here in Germany. When he heard that his friend's offer included a clean and rent-free place to live, plus a small sum of cash under the table, he moved willingly. Pavel remembered his friends and took care of them. Yevgeny knew the work he did here was menial, yet his friend paid him well enough. Although not a religious man, Yevgeny prayed silently to some vague god. "Remember Pavel. Keep him safe."

The old building wasn't far from his apartment and he could walk there in any weather. He was so close, that even if he had a bike, he wouldn't need it. Anatoly and Gennady were driving up again this afternoon. He appreciated spending the brief time with his old comrades, even if all they did was stand around in the cold and reminisce while they shared sips of the Moskovskaya vodka they brought him. It was a shame none of them had achieved their life's goals after their service to Mother Russia. Only Pavel had. And now he employed the three of them.

Within minutes of leaving his apartment, he had opened the gate and entered the warehouse office. As he waited for them, he studied once again the dog-eared photo of his friends. The four of them in their uniforms. Pavel, Anatoly, Gennady and Yevgeny. They were young then and their friendship had bonded through the brotherhood of military service. Yevgeny smiled warmly, blissfully unaware.

▪ ▪ ▪ ▪ ▪

Anatoly and Gennady did not mind the drive. The big bench seat of their white box truck accommodated their bulky frames just fine. They were quiet in their own ways and did not need frivolous conversation to be comfortable on the long ride. They were soldiers and knew how to wait.

They had worked together for years supporting the German Stasi in East Berlin, and before that in the Russian Army. Together since their basic training, they could pretty much anticipate each other's thoughts. The cabin of the truck was filled with a grey fog as they smoked and drove wordlessly. The dead arms of skeletal trees along the roadway saluted as they passed.

Gennady broke the silence, his leather jacket creaking as he turned to his friend. "We must take control of this and remove the Poles. They are spineless, whiny and weak. I am glad they do not know where our warehouse is Anatoly. They would turn on us without hesitation to save their own skins."

"Yes, Gennady, I know. Driving thirty-two kilometers to load the crates from their truck into ours and then bring them back to our warehouse is a nuisance. It would be much easier to have them deliver to our doors. But Pavel is right, keep these fools at arms' length. He will soon work out another way for us to get the deliveries and when that happens, the Poles are out." *Dead out*, Anatoly thought to himself.

As if reading Anatoly's mind Gennady said, "When the time comes, I want to kill that sniveling Karol. I will kill Tobiaz too if you like."

"We shall see, my brother. We shall see." Anatoly mused.

They continued in silence as they thought about the prospects. Anatoly knew that Pavel had specific plans for the Poles and they would be carried out only in the way he insisted.

The Russians had broken up their journey from Moscow to the warehouse in Warnemunde with an overnight in stop in Minsk. Cheap hotels were plentiful there, especially if they were willing to walk down the hall to a common bathroom. But on the trip back and with their load secure in the truck, they would drive straight through. There would be no stops unless one of them was with the truck at all times.

Anatoly had been told to take total control of the process. Pavel didn't mind how Anatoly accomplished that, but he wanted end-to-end control. That would mean the Poles had to be taken out of the loop.

Anatoly thought about it over and over. Pavel insisted he did not want the Poles to know the location of the Warnemunde Warehouse. This would be so much easier if Pavel would just tell him and Gennady where the guns were stashed. Then they could control the shipment from start to finish. Pavel however, wasn't ready for that. Anatoly knew that Pavel did not want to share the location of the cache with anyone he didn't have to, even with him. It bothered Anatoly that after all these years together, Pavel still didn’t trust him. Pavel’s way was a bit more complicated, but it was his decision. He liked complete control and didn't tolerate any loose ends.

As if to emphasize the need for the smallest group of trusted players, Pavel had made another decision. And this one also fell to Anatoly. He had to clean up a loose end.

■ ■ ■ ■ ■

Tobiaz locked the rear doors open against the side of their truck. His brother Karol looked in his rearview mirror and edged the rear bumper slowly against the dock sill. He hopped out and the two Poles climbed the slippery steel steps and entered the drafty building. Once winter set in, it never got warm in their terminal in Rostock. Cold and damp conditions were a way of life in these old empty structures, but this one served their purpose.

The building sat a few dozen kilometers south of Warnemunde. It had been abandoned since the Soviet Union disbanded and the East German economy, bad as it was, became worse. Tobiaz doubted he would live long enough to see it rebound. For now, they needed the warehouse, just a few hours from their Polish border, to transfer part of their load to the Russians before heading home.

"These guys scare me Tobiaz. I hate having

to meet with them. They bring nothing but trouble and we take all the risk. We don't need them," Karol whispered. The fall of their boots echoed loudly against the cold concrete walls.

Tobiaz responded in a whisper also, not that anyone could hear them in 10,000 square feet of empty storage space. "We have our orders Karol. If we want to continue with our own business, we must accommodate Gennady and Anatoly too. Let's just get this over with. They are connected, and they get paid to just show up. Once we leave, we can figure out what to do about it. Right now, we have just enough time to unload before they get here. You get back in the truck and I will get the lift-stacker. As soon as I get the crates off, pull the truck around back. I do not want them to see it."

Tobiaz went inside and pulled the dirty chain on the overhead door. Its tired springs groaned with the effort of being opened and the building braced itself for the blast of cold air that entered. There was never any heat on in the place, but it got even colder when the door opened and the wind blew in. Tobiaz hoped the Russians would come soon. He could not stand waiting in the cold. His hands and feet already ached as his blood receded from them. He knew it was to protect his vital organs from danger, as much as from the cold, but the knowledge did nothing to warm him.

They made short work of unloading the Russians' crates and Karol pulled their truck around back. He did not relish his next encounter with the Russians. Truth be told, he hated it.

■ ■ ■ ■ ■

The Poles' Rostock warehouse wasn't easy to find unless one knew where to look. It was an obscure, empty looking building in an unobtrusive, nearly abandoned neighborhood. Broken windows on the second story stared blindly onto the streets below. Anatoly pulled through the open gate, backed up near the loading dock and honked twice.

Inside, Tobiaz heard the horn and looked out through the dirty wired-glass window in the steel door, confirming it was the Russians. If they just stayed in their truck, it would be easier. Karol could load their crates directly into the back and they could be gone. The less contact with these two, the better. He nodded to Karol who pulled the chains that opened the overhead door. He saw the looming figure and recognize Gennady as he got out and opened the rear doors of the truck, folding them back along the sides. Anatoly backed the tail of the truck to the dock sill. Then he got out of the truck and headed for the door to the warehouse. *Fuck,* Tobiaz thought as he nodded to Karol to load the crates onto the truck. Karol, with one crate already on the forklift, pushed it into the back of the white box truck.

Anatoly's boots thudded heavily as he approached Tobiaz. Tobiaz could make out the obvious shape of the 9mm Makarov outlined under Anatoly's leather jacket. It was as if Anatoly wanted Tobiaz to see it. He guessed Gennady was similarly armed. If Anatoly's point was to make him feel afraid, he had succeeded.

This had been a simple operation until the Russians came into the mix. The last three transfers had been fraught with tension and it did not sit well with the two Polish brothers. The Russians were boorish and argumentative. They acted as if they owned the routes and the cargo.

A while back, Tobiaz's cousin, Tadeusz, had outlined a simple way to pick up and deliver additional goods at the plant in Reinbeck for a new buyer. Tadeusz and his German brother-in-law, Ulrich, would drive the goods from Reinbeck to this warehouse in Rostock and unload a new crate onto another truck. Simple as that.

Before the Russians, it was even simpler. Tadeusz and Ulrich would meet Tobiaz and

Karol near the Polish border at Kolbaskowo and transfer the crates there. Tobiaz and Karol would then proceed, with the stolen cigarettes and liquor, to their small garage at home in Szczecin, just inside the Polish border. It had been a simple movement of goods without danger.

The best part was Tadeusz's employer had been providing all the required documents to pass through customs at the border crossings. This business with the Russians was too complicated, with the extra stops and working with strangers. Strangers who had a demanding and aggressive style that bordered on threatening. And that worried Tobiaz.

He also worried for his younger brother Karol, who was a nice and quiet man, but also the fearful type. Gennady scared him terribly. Truth be told, he scared Tobiaz too. Gennady was a surly man with an angry personality. He reminded Tobiaz of an unemployed Stasi grunt. And his armed partner was standing right in front of him.

There was no greeting from Anatoly. The Russian started right in, "There has been change of plans," he growled. "Next time there is shipment for me, I ride with you to pick it up. Your brother will wait here with Gennady until we return. The customer wants to make sure there is no chance to interrupt delivery if something happens to one or both of you. So, I am now backup driver."

Tobiaz was stunned. "No Anatoly. That will not work. There is no need for back up drivers. If we need a backup, we will arrange it. The people on my other end will not be pleased with new faces. And if I must say it, I will. They will not be pleased to meet uninvited Russians as part of their operation. This is a family thing and you are not family."

Tobiaz was wary. This felt awfully bad deep inside, but he knew there was nothing he could do about it. He was in over his head. Smuggling cigarettes and booze had started as a nearly foolproof way to subsidize his meager truck driver's income. Now it had degraded into being told what to do by Russians, likely connected to the mafia in Moscow.

The outside door creaked as Gennady entered the plant. Anatoly's gaze never left Tobiaz, but Tobiaz looked past Anatoly's beefy shoulder. Yes, he confirmed there was the bulge of a gun under Gennady's jacket also.

Gennady looked at Tobiaz and Anatoly squaring off and looked directly at Tobiaz as he asked, "Problem?" That simple word was more a threat than a question.

Anatoly replied, "No Gennady, go close the

truck doors. We are done here." Then he turned to Tobiaz and said. "This is not up for debate. You will drive me with you next time. No?" Without waiting for an answer, he turned his back on the Poles and walked out.

As much as he wanted to, Tobiaz knew this was not the time to argue further. He merely nodded to the exiting form of the big Russian as Karol put the other crate onto their truck. The moment the Russians left the lot, Tobiaz locked the warehouse and the brothers headed for Szczecin.

Anatoly and Gennady left the parking lot and were well north onto Highway 103 before Gennady spoke. "We really need to kill them Anatoly. They are a problem that will not go away by itself."

"Yes, my friend. But for now, we need them. And if they are to be killed, Pavel will tell us when and how. Once the other drivers know me, they make delivery directly to us and we have eliminated one step. Then you can kill them both. Right now, we must get crates to warehouse."

Anatoly drove in silence a bit before he continued. "There is another matter. Now let us go see our friend Yevgeny."

■ ■ ■ ■ ■

Although they had not asked, Yevgeny had turned on the heat for his friends and the building was finally warming up. He heard their truck before he saw it. He opened the side door and came down the steps to meet them as they backed to the loading dock. The cold wind coming out of the northwest blew right down the canal and into his coat. Damn it was cold. He turned up his collar and held it tightly around his neck to keep the wind out. "Anatoly, Gennady. It is good to see you my friends."

Anatoly hopped down from the cab of the truck and hugged is old friend. Gennady came around and shook Yevgeny's hand heartily. For a brief moment Yevgeny noticed there was no hug. "Let us get these inside," Gennady said. "It is too cold to be out here."

Yevgeny returned to the inside of the building and pulled the chains that opened the overhead door. Anatoly backed the truck up while Gennady pushed the hydraulic pallet stacker in place. Within a few short minutes the truck was empty and the pallets sat next to two steel tables. They set about prying open the wooden crates immediately. Neither acknowledged the building's warmth nor spoke to Yevgeny, who watched from a distance, so as not to be in the way.

"Here is a list of what goes to Minsk,

Gennady. The items may have been put in either crate. Stack the Minsk pieces on the table so I can count them before we re-pack them. They have given us a shipping manifest that will get the crate into Belarus without alerting customs."

Anatoly and Gennady worked quietly as Yevgeny watched them carefully lay the guns on the table. He secretly lusted over the Makarov *pistolets*, and boxes and boxes of 9mm rounds, and the Kalashnikov rifles and their ammo. The cold steel glistened as the pieces were stripped of their cosmoline lubricant paper, examined and then re-wrapped. The power and quality of the weapons were not lost on him, even though he could never afford one.

Gennady picked up a Makarov and held it in his hand as if feeling the weight and balance of it. He nodded in approval and then opened an ammo box. He fed two rounds into a well-oiled magazine and worked the slide one time. All three of the friends appreciated the smooth metallic sound of a round being chambered. "Here Yevgeny," he said, "This one is for you." Yevgeny looked at his old friend, his eyes brimming with tears of gratitude. Smiling back in return, Gennady shot his friend twice in the face.

When the ringing cleared from Anatoly's ears he told Gennady, "When we finish here, weigh him down and roll him onto the canal. And be sure to grab his keys to this place. Pavel will want to know we now manage the warehouse and that we have eliminated this loose end for him."

Chapter Two

I WAS SITTING IN A THIN, TWO HUNDRED and two-foot aluminum tube atop one hundred seventy-six thousand pounds of fuel. I and another ninety-nine passengers paid five thousand dollars, more or less, to fly the Concorde across the Atlantic Ocean, at sixty thousand feet, in three and a half hours. I didn't personally pay the five grand. My company forked it over to buy my bulkhead seat. They wanted me in Germany "yesterday," as I was told. But yesterday I was in Detroit, so I was already a day late.

My wife and I had been driving back from Detroit to our home in New Jersey when I got the call. We had just left the funeral of my good friend, former police department partner and mentor. I found out on Monday that he had passed away and the funeral was the next day. We hopped in the car and made the ten-hour trip from our home in New Jersey to Detroit to attend the funeral service.

Along the way my wife contracted a pretty severe sinus infection. She was resting in the passenger seat beside me as we headed home. We were on the Interstate just inside the Pennsylvania state line from Ohio when my mobile phone rang loudly, breaking the silence. It startled us both. "This is Mike," I answered.

"Mike, this is Marianne." It was my CEO's executive assistant. "Where are you?" she asked. It was more of a demand than a question.

I wasn't sure and explained that I was traveling back to New Jersey somewhere along I-80. "Where on I-80 are you?" she asked immediately. "What's this all about," I asked, heading off her question. She replied, "Mr. Brinton needs you in Germany—right now."

Barry Brinton was her boss and "right now" was the way he lived. Everything was right now, and he meant it. I saw him immediately fire a group president who said "right now" was impossible.

I told Marianne I would be back in New Jersey in about five or six hours and could be at the office and leave from there in the morning. She then asked where I was relative to the nearest major airport. I guessed Pittsburgh.

"Fine," she said. "Head straight there. We'll have a company Gulf Stream meet you. I'll make arrangements for your car." The Gulf Stream could get me at least to London non-stop without refueling, but it was expensive. Something big was up.

"Alice is with me, Marianne, and she is really sick. I need to get her home and to a doctor or possibly a hospital."

"No," Marianne replied. "I'll get her home or to her doctor. You make it to the Fixed Base Operator at the airport in Pittsburgh." The FBO was where private aircraft came and went, bypassing the crowds and gate security. I had used plenty of them traveling around the world as global security executive for this Fortune 25 Company.

"No, Marianne, I'll go home and make arrangements for my wife from there. She's too sick for me to just drop her off at an airport with people she doesn't know."

Working for the CEO, Marianne wasn't used to the word *No*. I knew my career was on the line, but at this point, it was what it was. She said, "I'll get back with you," and abruptly hung up.

A few minutes later, she called back and said "We'll have a driver at your home when you get there. Be ready to leave immediately. As far as Mr. Brinton is concerned, you are already a day late." And she hung up again. There it was. Her tone had a foreboding sense of finality to it. I am sure Brinton had come across the same way to her. She wasn't used to telling him that someone said no to him. And he wasn't used to hearing it either.

I goosed the engine to about ninety miles per hour and got home in record time. A stretch-limo had backed up the winding driveway and sat facing the street behind our friend Cindy's car. She had agreed by phone, without hesitation, to take care of my wife and meet us at the house. Her husband worked for the same company I did and they both understood "right now."

I leaned into the limousine driver's window and asked where in Germany I was going. "No idea," he replied, "but we need to leave immediately for the airport." Newark airport was easily an hour from my home.

I ran into the house with my wife, gave her a kiss, grabbed my "go-bag" with a couple sets of undies, two folded shirts, a clean pair of slacks, my extra toiletries and headed back out the door.

I climbed in the open back door of the limo and the driver closed it quickly, practically jumping into the front seat as he sped down the curving driveway to the street. “Where are we going?” I asked.

“I have no idea where you are going, but I am to get you to Kennedy Airport in New York and we have less than two hours. Your tickets and briefing should be in here, I would think.” With that, he handed me a sealed manila envelope.

I poured a whiskey over some ice from the bar in back and sipped the contents as I tried reading. I could sense that he was seriously breaking the speed limit as we flew down every street and highway. Kennedy Airport was every bit of two hours away, and that was if we encountered no traffic.

I read quickly. My journey would take me from New York to London, to Hamburg, and then by car to Reinbeck, Germany. My first-class ticket was already in the envelope. It would take me about as long to get the six hundred miles from London to Hamburg as it would the thirty-five hundred miles from New York to London. The Concorde flew supersonically at twice the speed of sound in the middle layer of the stratosphere.

Our European General Counsel had written the summary for me. It was tight, crisp and informative. The envelope contained her notes on key employees, including a senior vice president who ran the operations in Reinbeck.

Wilhelm Warner was an engineering Ph.D. who preferred to be called "Doctor" by everyone. It also contained the summary of the German federal prosecutor's interviews with our counsel and her team. As I read, the story and the need for urgency became clear.

Over the past several months, the German Federal Prosecutor had been secretly conducting an investigation into the smuggling of contraband from Germany into Poland. The ring was only fairly sophisticated, allegedly using our company trucks and cargo manifests as Customs clearance documents. The government suspected employees of our Reinbeck plant as complicit in the conspiracy.

The plant works-union had advised its member employees to band together in a circle of silence. They refused to answer any of the prosecutor's inquiries. Fourteen hundred employees all kept mum. Furthermore, the plant manager pleaded helplessness in his ability to sway the union or the employees into cooperation. Warner also told the prosecutor he was barking up the wrong tree, saying that regardless of his information and his investigative leads, it was impossible that such activity could occur without him or his management team being aware of it. The prosecutor and his chief investigator took the resistance as a stall tactic, possible complicity in the crimes and a personal affront to their investigation.

In retaliation for the lack of even minimal cooperation, the prosecutor seized the plant and closed it, idling fourteen hundred workers. One of the largest employers in the region, idled. Parts for Germany's largest manufacturers of automobiles, motor coaches, buses, trains and trucks were no longer being delivered "just in time," as our contracts required.

After being closed only three days, our company had technically breached its contractual delivery terms with several of our largest customers. Penalties for contractual non-performance were now coming in at over two million dollars per day. No wonder my company did not want me delaying my departure by even twelve hours. It didn't matter that this had gotten out of hand on someone else's watch. It didn't matter that our European Counsel let this slip out of her control. It didn't matter that the plant manager had a labor problem and a government-relations problem of his own doing. The matter was now in my hands as so many had been before. And the clock was running.

At the bottom of the last page of my briefing notes was a large hand-written scrawl that I recognized. It was from our CEO. "*Fix This!*" he wrote. I was soon to learn that "*this*" was even more complicated than anyone expected.

So, there I was, on my first trip on the Concorde and I was excited. I was no stranger to corporate travel. I had flown many corporate aircraft, from Cessna fixed-wing prop planes to luxurious corporate jets with stand-up showers in the bathroom, to two-seat helicopters and six-passenger, leather-trimmed Bell executive copters with flight attendants. But the Concorde was big-time.

This bird was a monster aircraft. In order to take off, it had to be cart-driven to the farthest end of the longest runway at JFK International Airport. Once there it was backed up facing east against a retaining wall tall enough for the jet engines to push against. Prior to take off, the flight engineer announced over the loudspeaker system what we should expect during the takeoff sequence. He prefaced it by saying "You will experience a lot of engine noise and a great deal of shuddering from the aircraft. This is perfectly normal. Even though it may seem like it, the parts will not fall off."

He went on to explain that the plane achieved its optimum efficiency when flying in the layer of the atmosphere where there was the least air resistance.

The long nose of the plane was shaped like a rocket and it interfered with pilot visibility. So, Air France developed the moveable nose. During take off and landing, the nose was hydraulically angled downward to provide visibility for the crew. Once airborne, the nose was raised again to give it the streamlined design it needed to make it a virtual rocket.

I recall thinking during take off how loud the engine noise was inside the cabin, and that the pilot might have been optimistic about nothing falling off. The entire crew must have been standing on the brakes as the engines revved up and the plane shuddered terribly as it gained thrust power.

Finally, they released the brakes and the plane seemed to crawl down the runway. On and on we rolled to gain the speed necessary to lift that baby. I had never been on a takeoff that lasted so long and worried that we might end up rolling off the runway and dive into Head of Bay Basin. Finally, I could feel the nose lift off the ground, but it seemed like it was taking forever to get the rest of that bird in the air. The plane emitted a terrible sound on the ground and it didn't abate once it got in the air.

Once airborne, we accelerated to cruising

altitude at a very steep angle for the longest time, shaking and shuddering the entire way. Just before the nose was returned to its normal angle, the pilot made an announcement telling us he was going to do so. He also said that although the engines would be operating just fine, we would soon not hear them. He told us not to worry, we would be traveling at twice the speed of our own sound. Down below, on the Atlantic Ocean, sonic booms would be occurring along our flight path.

Sure enough, once we became a rocket, the engine sound in the cabin was gone. It was eerily quiet. There was a flight-tracker on a screen mounted on the bulkhead wall. It was the strangest thing to see how fast the plane's icon was moving across the screen toward our destination. Once the plane stabilized at altitude, the flight attendants served us a wonderful five-star surf and turf meal with absolutely no turbulence. It was like sitting in a fancy restaurant, with the seating only a bit tighter. Very nice touch. I felt fortunate for the experience.

■ ■ ■ ■ ■

At London's Heathrow Airport, crowds gathered on the airport balconies to watch the spectacle of this beast taxiing to its gate. I didn't have enough time for a quick nap during the layover but managed a sandwich before boarding the Lufthansa flight to Hamburg.

My plane from London got into Hamburg at about five in the afternoon, local time. The place was packed with commuters. As I deplaned through customs I looked around and saw a chauffeur near the ground transportation doors. He was holding a sign with my last name and the initials for my company name. I nodded as our eyes met. He introduced himself as Friedrich, quickly shook my hand as he grabbed my carry-on bag and rushed me to his car. He had a sliced apple, some cheese chunks, grapes and a piece of fresh crusty bread on a platter in the car. "There is coffee, water and beer in the refrigerator. There is wine in the shelf," he said in heavily German-accented English. "We will be in the car only a short while. You might sleep a half hour." I thought about it. It had been over twenty-four hours since I had any sleep and I was planning to head right to the plant.

I ate a bit and enjoyed the wonderful baked bread and nutty cheese flavors more than the grapes. I didn't bother with the apple. I felt sluggish but was too tired to sleep so I reread the briefing notes for the third time. This time I tried to understand it, not from the perspective of the plant and its impact on our bottom line, our lawyers, or the customers. This time I read it from the viewpoint of the federal prosecutor. He was the only one who could give us back our plant. What kind of case did he have and what did he really want?

I put myself in his shoes, travelling back nearly fifteen years to when I had been a prosecutor's investigator in the elite Wayne County Organized Crime Task Force in Detroit. There I was on a team of investigators and prosecutors who worked major criminal conspiracies. My mentor and partner who had just passed away, was an expert in the theft and international fencing of automotive equipment and precious industrial metals. Sitting at his knee, I learned how people and materials are only permitted to cross international borders by meeting certain protocols. Neither customs inspectors nor border patrol agents would typically ignore these rules. But somewhere, some business insider was involved. Someone had to give the wink and the nod, had to look the other way, to forge papers or dummy up a manifest. A guard, an employee, or a dockworker—someone had to help. There were other ways too, but they usually involved ignorance or extremely poor internal controls. Our company was not known for weak internal controls. Not by a long shot.

I ate and read and drank coffee from the hot thermos Friedrich provided me as he expertly navigated our route.

As it turned out my flight arrived too late for the plant management team to meet me so we drove to my hotel. The Waldhaus was a small, old-style, stone-architecture inn with only a dozen or so rooms. The slate-roofed lodge was over a hundred years old. If I had more time, I would have asked for a guided tour of the place. It was beautiful in a historic sense. It was once an inn that provided nourishment for members of a local hunt club.

It survived the British and US shuttle bombing raids of World War II, much like my company's nearby plant had before we acquired it. In the early 1940s, the manufacturing facility cranked out tanks for Rommel's German Armored divisions in Africa. Hidden in the woods and under a canopy of thick, hundred-year-old trees, the plant was not visible from the sky. Today, it cranked out parts for nearly everything that rolled in Europe. Well, not today. Today the plant was closed, and my job was to *Fix This.*

I dropped my bag on the bed, stripped out of my clothes, and took a long hot shower. I slipped on some fresh underwear and the heavy white cotton robe provided by the hotel. I wanted to look relatively rested and not feel as though I had been in my clothes for the past two days, even though I had. I finished the fruit and washed it down with a pot of strong, but sweet German coffee with cream. I usually have it black, but the Germans have mastered the art of removing the bitterness from their coffee and like it sweet with milk, *Siesse muss d'r Coffe sein—Milchkaffee*. I ate, read and finished the pot.

I thought I would read myself to sleep. But between the caffeine and the weight of this problem, that didn't happen. That and the fact that it was still the early part of the afternoon by my body clock and I was too wired. So, I wrote notes about the plant's operations. I covered everything, from receiving raw materials to shipping finished product. I drew a couple slightly different process flow charts. I wanted to include some variables based on manufacturing and assembly that may be unique to automotive parts plants, compared with plants that we owned which built aircraft parts. The company also produced goods for government contracts, including classified items for military and other government customers. I sent a quick email to my office and confirmed that this facility was not bound by any such government secrecy requirements—one less thing to worry about.

■ ■ ■ ■ ■

A cold but bright sun had just risen, and I was still without an hour's sleep. I dressed and walked outside to get some morning air before calling my driver. Friedrich was already waiting at the car, leaning alongside the rear passenger door. Either he had not gone to his home or office last night or had just arrived back. I doubted he had waited the last ten hours for me. He opened the rear door as I approached. "I'll sit in the front," I told him.

He smiled and politely said, "Nein. You must arrive in the back, please." So, I did.

It was an interesting ride to the plant. The main roads were tree lined and many were paved with cobblestones that looked like they had just been swept. As heavy as the traffic was, I didn't hear a single car horn honked in frustration. Rush hour had begun, and I watched the bustle of a brisk industrial community, where the residents of this small charming town all drove to work simultaneously and courteously. I was glad I had re-read the file a few hours earlier. It would have been difficult with the stop-and-go motion of the Mercedes limousine, even in all its corporate opulence.

When we pulled up to the plant, I observed the access control process at the entry gate to the walled-in facility. The driver, who seemed to know the security officer, still had to undergo a display of his license and I was asked to show my passport as well as my business card. I must have been already on the approved visitor list because as soon as he saw my name, the guard brought his boot heels to a clacking snap. He briefly stood at attention as he raised the security gate and waived us through. My driver looked at me through the rear-view mirror, raised his eyebrows in a sense of curiosity and then smiled. He took me directly to what was obviously the plant administrative office building.

There was a very small welcoming party waiting for me under the covered veranda of a red, stone building. Perfectly set slate tiles covered the roof and I envisioned German craftsmen laying them neatly in place. From the personnel files in my briefing envelope I recognized Doctor Wilhelm Warner, the top guy at this facility, as one of the two greeters. I exited the back seat as my door was officiously opened. With my left hand I presented my business card, extended my other hand and warmly said "Doctor Warner, a pleasure."

Warner advised me the pronunciation of his name was "Vaerner. Vilhelm Vaerner." He then limply shook my hand. It seemed as if I had just wiped something unclean with it and he could barely stand to touch it. "Let us go inside," he said.

The inside of the building appeared never to have been renovated but gleamed immaculately. Inside Warner's office, there wasn't a speck on the polished floor or a piece of paper not parallel to the lines of the desk it rested on. Warner's guest chairs sat at forty-five-degree angles, cornered to his desk—precisely. There were no family pictures on his walls, desk or credenza. His diplomas and professional certifications seemed to be his family. They were everywhere, as if he needed to remind himself of his importance. Each wall had some document with an official seal. One wall had several arranged in matching frames, one under the other, in date order. And every edge aligned perfectly. His was a compulsive mind that needed a place for everything, and everything had to be correctly in its place. Warner was a sequential processor who had to be in charge. He would not do well managing change, much less chaos. He motioned for me to sit in the seat opposite his desk. I noted that his chair was elevated to its highest setting, a power play to establish control. I used the technique myself in interrogations. I decided this was not yet an interrogation, so I sat, falling low into a soft leather cushion. Very comfortable, but quite beneath Werner's perch. Just the way he planned it.

"So, please Mr. Christian, tell me why you are here." He sat looking down at me, with his elbows on his desk. His pink fingertips formed a neatly manicured steeple, covering his thin lips yet barely grazing his perfectly groomed mustache. I could not believe, since he was there to greet me, that he was ignorant of who I was or why I had been sent. I decided it was time to establish the ground rules.

"Doctor *Warner,"* I began, pronouncing it his way. "In case you haven't noticed, your parking lot is empty. Your plant is empty. No workers are staffing your lines. No trucks are moving in or out of your plant. No inventory is being shipped to *our* customers. And this inactivity at *your* plant is costing our company over two million US dollars a day. I have been sent here to fix this."

"But you are just a security person." He said, "security person" as if it were a dirty word. "You are not a lawyer or an engineer. This is a waste of our time—your time and most importantly MY time," he huffed. "I have met with you as I have been instructed. Now I am leaving. You should too. This is a matter to be handled in Germany. Not by the States, and certainly not by a *security person.*" He stood as if to indicate the meeting was over. There it was again. The disdain.

I rose but did not move from in front of my chair. "Doctor Warner, here is a phone number. I was told if you had trouble with my presence here, you should call this number." I passed along another of my business cards onto which I wrote a phone number.

He tossed the card onto his desk without reading it. "I do not need to call anyone. This is my plant."

"No," I firmly said. "This is not *your* plant." I hit the word *your* really hard, to make my point. "This plant belongs to the Company. It is in the responsible care of the Chief Executive Officer of the Company on behalf of its shareholders. You are merely its custodian. And you have let production here grind to a halt, all because of alleged crimes that can neither be proved nor disproved by you. I am here to fix this and you are now to call that number."

"Who is this at the number? Who am I to call?" he asked. I knew I had him. If he was as confident as he was making out to be, he would have tossed the card into his wastebasket and walked me to the door. He did not.

"This is the personal phone number to your boss's boss. Now call him." I said.

"No, I think it is not necessary to bother him." Warner's voice was quiet. Not out of a sense of respect for Brinton being disturbed at three o'clock in the morning, but because he was losing his certainty about his position of power.

"No, Doctor Warner." I said. "You no longer have an option. Call him now or I will."

The color began to drain from Warner's face. He had boxed himself into a corner by trying to bully me. As he raised the card to read the numbers, I noticed his fingers were shaking. "This really isn't necessary ..." he began.

"We are past that now Doctor. Call the number."

Warner stood at his desk. He dialed from his desk phone but did not put it on the speaker. I didn't need to hear what was being said, I had seen this acted out before, and it wasn't going to be pretty for Warner.

Warner must have recognized the U.S. area code as that of New Jersey, our Corporate Headquarters location. And he knew it was very early in the States. "Guten Morgen. This is Doctor *Vaerner*. I am so sorry to bother you, but I was told I had to call you." He paused.

"Well yes, perhaps I did convey that impression. Yes, he did tell me why he was here, but ..." Warner's jaw clamped shut. He stood practically at attention as he listened. Then he began to flush angrily, and the color deepened in his jowls and the back of his neck. I could hear the sound of words on the other end, but could not make out what was being said. I didn't need to know.

Then his head sagged, his jaw almost touched his chest. “Yes, sir.” he said quietly. “Yes, I understand.” Then he abruptly stood taller. “The whole plant? But he is not a Doctor. He is not even an engineer. He is just a security per…”

I could hear the words now, right through Warner’s earpiece. “HE IS IN CHARGE OF EVERYTHING! Do what he says. He speaks for me.”

“Yes, sir.” But I knew that Warner was speaking to a disconnected phone at that point.

Warner looked at me in complete disbelief, and in complete surrender. He looked crushed. I knew I could drive him into further submission or try to save him. I guessed my boss was already having two sets of papers drawn up. One set included a separation package for an executive termination. The other for a demotion to some obscure responsibility, in some even more obscure country. That would be unacceptable to such an egotist as Warner. But if he quit he would lose all separation pay and bonuses. Either way, Warner was a short timer and he knew it. The best he could hope for would be to mitigate his damages. And cooperating with me, as distasteful as that must have seemed, was his path to success.

"What do you want? How can I help you?" he asked. It was as simple as that. He should have opened with it.

"I want you to call in the head of the works-union. I want to see him immediately. I want to see all production orders and run cycles and all non-standard customer orders from the last sixty days. I want to see all inventory records for parts that sat on the shelf over forty-five days and records of all sales. I want to see all security logs of vehicles entering and leaving and I want copies of all video of the gates for vehicles leaving and entering for the last sixty days. I want a list of all your drivers and dock loaders. I want the manifests for all cross-border shipments for the last sixty days. I will need this information before lunch."

He did not start out taking notes, but now Warner was scribbling furiously. "I will need three offices with telephones," I continued. "And in each office, I want computers connected to the company network and two of them separately connecting to the Internet. I will need computer passwords and visitor passes for myself and some people I am bringing in. There will be three others to begin with. They will be here this afternoon before dinner. I want us all to have twenty-four-hour, all-access badges to all areas, and three vehicle passes. Tell your key staff and security people that whatever we ask for, they are to provide it, including access to all areas. They are to give us any documents, statements and interviews we request."

"I also want you to arrange for me to meet the Federal Prosecutor. I want the meeting today, preferably over lunch. I want the meeting at a quiet place, neither his turf nor ours. That is why I want a restaurant. He is to bring his lead investigator on this case. The meeting will likely last not more than two hours. That should help him plan. When he asks who I am, tell him I am the man sent here to fix this for him. Be sure to say I am fixing it 'for him.' Do not take no for an answer."

"Should I plan to attend also?" asked Warner.

"No, that will not be necessary at this time. Now I need a fully equipped office."

"Take mine", Warner said dejectedly.

I felt a bit guilty. "No, I said, that will not be necessary."

"Oh, yes, it is necessary. I was told on the call to give you my office."

"OK," I said. Simple as that. I grabbed my briefcase and moved behind his desk, setting the case on it as I sat. I did not lower the seat. "Let us begin." And I nodded him to the door to get started on my list.

Chapter Three

IT WAS ALMOST ONE-THIRTY IN THE morning as Tobiaz drove with Anatoly to the Pole's little warehouse in Rostock. They had jumped off Highway 103 taking neighborhood roads to Lubecker-strasse, crossing the railroad tracks where the street ended in an industrial area. The empty warehouse was just a half block from the harbor inlet. The water was deep enough for ships, but the wharf area had long been bereft of commercial traffic. There were no large vessels at these small docks, just a fishing boat in disrepair. A few slips up they could see two tugs sitting idle and unattended. Bubbles circulated beneath the waterline to keep them from freezing into the water.

Tobiaz would have to relocate to another warehouse soon. The buildings in this area were being condemned to make way for hotels and tourist attractions. The waterfront property was becoming more valuable for trade in tourism than in commerce. Tobiaz could feel the cold down in his bones, and being with Anatoly, the overwhelming darkness of the warehouse district made it seem colder. Having to share the knowledge of his location with Anatoly complicated things. And having to introduce him to Tadeusz just made it worse.

"There it is," said Tobiaz nodding to the white box truck. The engine was running. "Tadeusz will be driving. He is my aunt's son and works at the plant in Reinbeck. He should be with Ulrich. We are related to him because he is married to Tadeusz's sister. It is Ulrich who has the company connection to the manifests we use. Try to be nice, please Anatoly. We all want this to work well."

Anatoly grunted. "I do not need to be your relative Tobiaz. And I do not want to be anyone's friend. As far as they are concerned I am backup driver, sent here by customer to ensure uninterrupted delivery. They need only to know that."

Tobiaz could not wait to get the load from Tadeusz into his truck and get on their way. He never felt in such a foul mood as when he was with the Russians.

When the opportunity first arose, the route and goods they were delivering were pretty simple. His cousin stole cases of cigarettes and liquor without tax stamps from local, bonded distribution warehouses. He then brought them to the plant.

At the plant, the goods were placed in cardboard cartons and packed into a shipping crate. A customs manifest was generated for the crate as a one-off delivery. Legitimate customer orders were loaded onto their truck along with their “special delivery” cargo. All the paperwork was in order for them to leave the plant.

Tadeusz and Ulrich would then drive the goods to their Rostock warehouse. Tobiaz and Karol would then load the cargo onto their own truck and move the goods into Poland for sale. Their routine was smooth and worked well for them all.

From customs paperwork, to multiple border crossings, to highway checkpoints there was no problem because the weights, measures and contents in the sealed crates were all accounted for on paper.

It was all going pretty well, that is, until they were told to load another crate for delivery. This container they knew nothing about. The paperwork was also okay, and customs officials never questioned them. The company name was powerful, and their deliveries were so frequent that it was a nuisance to inspect. It was again, simple to execute, but nerve wracking for the cousins. Who was the crate for? What was in it? Why did this fall on them to deliver? If it hadn't been for the extra money, it would not be worth the worry to work with Russians, especially these Russians.

When Anatoly and Tobiaz arrived at the Rostock warehouse dock, Anatoly hopped out, ignoring Tadeusz and his truck. He pushed open the heavy gate and waited as Tobiaz pulled the truck inside. Ulrich's truck contained their crate and Anatoly's. Since the Russians had to pick up the crate on Tobiaz's turf, the Pole felt compromised.

They all had their suspicions about the extra crates. One guess was scrap metal being stolen from the plant and sold in Minsk. Another conjecture was that out-of-specification parts were being sold as OEM, or Original Equipment Manufacture, rather than being re-worked or scrapped. Someone else guessed that weapons or drugs were in the crates and being smuggled through Poland and into Kiev in the Ukraine. They didn't really know how close their guesses were, nor did they want to. What they did know was that the extra crate was very heavy and involved the use of a hydraulic lift-stacker on their truck to load and unload it. They never opened the Russians' crates. No one dared.

Tadeusz and Ulrich exited their truck.

"What is this?" Tadeusz asked, "Where is Karol? Who is this?"

As he predicted, Tobiaz knew that Tadeusz would not like this at all. He tried to put his best face forward.

"Karol is at the border waiting for us to return. This is Anatoly. We will be adding a backup driver to the route in case something happens to either Karol or me. The customer at the other end wants assurances that the shipments will continue, on schedule. I brought him along to introduce you and to show him the route."

"What do you mean another driver? We did not talk about this. I have many others who would like to drive for us. People we know. I cannot take him to the plant and just make him a driver. There is a process for that. I do not know this man Tobiaz. How do you come to know him?"

Anatoly was not going to let this get out of hand. "The customer appointed me. It is simple as that. I am regular driver on route now. Introduction is mere formality."

The moment he spoke, Tadeusz knew that

Anatoly was Russian. "A Russian? Tobiaz, are you mad? What are you thinking? I have Turks, Moldavians and Germans that I know and trust more than an unknown Russian. This cannot happen!"

Tobiaz felt that Tadeusz was right. But this was now out of his hands. The moment the Russians were introduced to this thing of theirs, it was out of his control.

"Tadeusz. This entire operation only succeeds if their customer is happy and willing to pay. And he pays so generously. More than we made on our own before. Now he has changed the terms of our agreement. He wants backup drivers and he has appointed this man. I was uncertain at first as well. But as Anatoly says, it is what the customer wants, and I am afraid it is not open for discussion."

Tadeusz was seeking a way around this arrangement. "What if we do not deliver anymore? What if it all ends right here, tonight. This will be the last shipment." Tobiaz saw Anatoly stiffen. He knew the Russian was armed and he seemed provoked and darkly angry.

Ulrich had been quiet up to until now. He seemed initially dazed by the turn of events. Now he spoke. "This is absurd. We have a deal. We have an arrangement. We set the terms, not the customer. If he wants his goods, he must live by our terms. He has nothing without us."

As if he had done it a thousand times, Anatoly reached behind his back and smoothly drew his Makarov and slipped it under Ulrich's chin. "The terms have changed. No?"

A wet stain was forming between Ulrich's legs. "No, I mean yes! The terms have changed. Please. Please. I have children."

Anatoly pressed the nose of the pistol hard into the soft flesh under Ulrich's jaw. "We have no more discussion. It is done. I am driver and I say what goes. Your next delivery is due on Tuesday. I drive truck with Tobiaz, or anyone I please. You will be here, or I will find you. Clear?" Ulrich was having trouble standing, much less answering.

Tadeusz and Tobiaz answered nearly simultaneously for him, "Yes. Yes. It is clear."

Anatoly released Ulrich who dropped to the ground holding his throat. There was sure to be a bruise.

"Now load my truck."

Tobiaz and Tadeusz backed their trucks up to adjacent docks. Ulrich and Anatoly stood outside. Neither spoke to the other and Anatoly was fine with that. He could care less about these Poles and Germans. And Ulrich was too sore and terrified to talk. *We should have seized all their land after the war,* Anatoly mused. The

Poles had split only recently, and the Berlin Wall was down less than a year. It was still in rubble in some places. *What a mistake. We should have killed them all.*

Tadeusz jumped onto the rear deck of his truck and operated the stacker. He gingerly raised Tobiaz's crate and backed it off the truck to the dock platform. He then carefully turned the forks and pushed the load into Tobiaz's truck. He repeated the process with the Russian's crate.

"Be careful!" barked Anatoly. The crates with the cigarettes and liquor were remarkably lighter. Each time, it was that damned mysterious crate that was so heavy and so worrisome to Tadeusz and Tobiaz. That cargo was the only one the Russians were interested in.

"Hurry with the other," Anatoly muttered, "I want to get going before dark." Once the Russian got his crates loaded onto his truck he could leave. He cared not for small talk.

Tadeusz and Ulrich would make their last parts delivery and then go home. *If it wasn't for such a large amount of cash, so regularly paid, I would give this up. If dealing with the Russians is a price I must pay, then I will do it,* Tobiaz thought. His wife liked the new lifestyle, the new car and a more regular supply of groceries for their boy and girl. She was now talking about a third child. She did not ask obvious questions and he blessed her for that.

Ulrich pulled down the overhead door on the truck. "I cannot wait to get out of here", he said over his shoulder as he walked away from the Russian.

Anatoly looked at Ulrich and could only see cross hairs between Ulrich's shoulder blades. *Good riddance,* he thought.

Tobiaz said an apologetic goodbye to Tadeusz and Ulrich and dropped his truck into low gear easing away from the dock doors. They would use the hand pallet stacker in the back of his truck to remove Anatoly's crates onto the Russian's truck, which was parked in a vacant lot a few buildings down. Anatoly did not want these other guys to ever see his truck relative to their warehouse.

It was still a couple hours to Szczecin. It would be dark when Tobiaz arrived and the sooner he could get rid of the Russian, the better. He rolled down the window as he reached over to open the door for the big Russian. "I am sorry for the way they behaved," he said to Anatoly. "They feel threatened by a stranger being added to the group."

"I told you. I do not care. I am not here to be friend to them or you."

Chapter Four

MY FIRST CALL WAS TO MY FRIEND WHO was also the owner of a global security-consulting firm I used for "special" resources, when I was overseas. Morgan Andercott was a former US Senate prosecutor's investigator who had worked several high-profile "special investigator" cases for Congress. Now he had his own global security services firm in New York.

"Morgan", I said into the phone when my call connected to his private mobile.

He recognized my voice. "Mike," he replied. "Where are you now?"

I thoroughly enjoyed our relationship. No bullshit when it came to business. We just got right to it. We saved the congeniality for when we got together in the City, at his place overlooking Central Park. His high-rise penthouse apartment had a view to die for. We'd have cocktails in his suite before dinner and talk about his family, my family, sports and world politics. I'd ask about some of his people I had met and worked with in the past. And there was always the traditional ritual of me turning down his standing offer to become a partner in his firm. After those pleasantries, there was the private elevator ride down to Tavern on the Green for more cocktails and light appetizers. But this was not New York City and we were not talking family here.

I briefed him. Told him the skillsets I thought I would need. We did not talk cost or timing and I knew he was not taking notes. He never did. "I will call you back in ten minutes," he said. "What's a good number?" I looked at the number on Warner's desk set and gave it to him before we disconnected.

I could hear Warner in the outer office talking loudly and fuming at someone on the other end of his phone conversation.

Warner hung up from his call and knocked on my new office door. He entered and explained, "I am having trouble. My accounting and controller managers are all off doing things at home while they are not working. My works-union leader will not come in unless we open the plant." He seemed satisfied with the explanation.

"Call them back right now. Tell each one they have only one choice to make. They will come in immediately, or you will fire them on that phone call. It is as simple as that. It's their only choice. If you cannot handle that, then I will fire you immediately. I can work with your plant engineer sitting out there to help me make those calls myself. How would you like to proceed?"

"I will do as you ask," was all he said. He turned, left my office and sullenly closed the door behind him. I could hear him talking quietly to the engineer. "What?" I heard him exclaim. Then they moved away talking in muted voices. I fully expected their people would show up within the hour and begin compiling the paper work I required.

I was hoping for more participation from these guys, some critical thinking and energy on their part, and I wasn't getting it. After all, they were in charge here. We needed results and needed them fast. It was almost as if they were oblivious of the impact this closure was having. The fact they could blame it on the German prosecutor seemed to take all pressure off of them to act with a sense of urgency. Our cost per hour was outrageous. It wasn't really *my* cost per hour, but the penalty cost per hour. At the current rate, without escalator clauses kicking in, it was costing nearly eight-five thousand dollars an hour, twenty-four hours a day, just in penalties.

I needed to impress the prosecutor. He needed to see there was a new kid in town. I wanted him to believe that the federal police, the *Bundespolizei*, had an ass kicker on their side.

Within a few moments, I got a callback from Morgan. He gave me the names of three guys who were already on their way to Reinbeck, all U.S. sounding names. They would be at the plant around three o'clock my time. That was perfect. Two were financial crimes investigators by civilian training and all three were combat arms specialists by military training. Even if they didn't burst through the documents at light speed, they would understand what we were looking for and know where to look for it.

Their task was to seek out anomalies, the redheaded stepchild that didn't fit in the family photo. They would identify the patterns in the business process that I laid out for them. Find the oddities that were universally recognized in self-dealing and in internal fraud. Those patterns would have owners and they would bring us our leads, if not our perpetrators.

Morgan also said he was lining up additional resources in case we needed to conduct a rolling surveillance. My first reaction was that the three guys should be plenty. I had run multiple surveillances and felt three would be adequate. But I had also learned over time, that when it came to my operations overseas, Morgan was infinitely more experienced with the nuances. I did not decline his suggestion.

I thanked him. He shrugged it off, as if mobilizing three qualified people a continent away in ten minutes was routine. This is why we did not talk price when I asked Morgan for resources. The man delivered, and you paid what it took for that kind of response.

I got out my briefing packet and re-read the European General Counsel's notes on the Federal Prosecutor. Young, forty, divorced, hard worker, tenaciously aggressive and single minded. Jaeger Felder had fast tracked from an assignment in Karlsruhe. An assignment that gained him visibility by leading a case supporting the United Nations in a multi-national arms smuggling investigation. Now he was involved with customs and border control issues. That explained why he was involved in this case. He was going after a high-profile, American corporation operating in Germany and Poland. A large company who was possibly involved in smuggling contraband across international borders.

Felder's lead investigator was only a little younger, but seasoned. Rutger Becker had rapidly moved from local police service in Berlin to a Federal posting after leading a series of high profile arrests. Local police have only limited policing authority but they are very well trained. From the day Becker hit the streets he established a network of informants that produced leads on everything from neo-Nazi gang activity to theft and fencing of industrial cargo. This got him noticed at the Federal level. On his first promotional examination after six years on the street as a Stadtpolizei, he scored remarkably high. He was invited and accepted a transfer and promotion into the federal Bundespolizei. In short order, Becker became Felder's lead investigator.

I surmised that Felder was looking for a high visibility solution to this case as another major milestone. Prosecute this successfully and land the next promotion. Being stonewalled by a works-union boss and a plant executive was not going to get him his fifteen minutes of fame. I was here to fix that. I had to help him solve this case. And I absolutely had to get my plant back online. Immediately.

As I leaned back I could hear the rich leather office chair creaking quietly. I felt my body start to relax. My eyes suddenly grew heavy and I was reminded how tired I was. I also knew how excited I was to throw myself into this. I thought back. Way back.

It seemed impossible to imagine that I was in Germany working on an international smuggling case involving cross-country diplomacy, foreign federal crimes, geopolitical relationships, fourteen hundred jobs hanging in the balance and two million dollars a day in penalties. If it weren't so serious, it would almost seem humorous that the fate of our business here in Reinbeck, and of our employees and customers, had been placed in my hands. Me, a former cop from Detroit. Maybe Warner was right. Maybe I was "just a security guy." But for some threats, I was the company fixer.

Things seemed to be moving, but too slowly. I was nowhere closer to solving this case than when I got in the limo at home less than twenty-four hours ago. I wanted Morgan's team on the ground fast. They would help me find that oddity that stood out. I planned to get a confession or some other break in this case. But right now, I didn't even have a suspect.

The quiet knock again. Warner stuck his head in. "Excuse me, Mr. Christian. I have called again as you instructed and told them what you said. They will be in shortly. All of them. But they are not happy." I figured that the message the employees got was that the new guy was going to fire them. Not Doctor Warner, the man in charge.

"Thank you. Now I would like you to bring me full aerial views of the plant, the plot plans as built, floor drawings and a production flow chart. I want to go over these with you."

"Yes sir," Warner said. There didn't seem to be any rancor in his voice. I think he was seeing positive activity towards problem solving and it fit in his comfort zone.

"And what did the federal prosecutor say?" I asked.

"He said he would get back with me later this morning." Warner replied. "At least he did not say no."

I frowned. "Remember what I said. *No* is not an option." I nodded to the door, encouraging him to get those prints and drawings for me. It would help to get a good visual of these mammoth grounds before I went outside to walk and ride them with my newly forming team.

I figured that Warner was more accustomed to giving orders than taking them and I guessed he did not know right where to go for the prints. He would have to ask the engineer for help with that and that would take even more time.

I got up to stretch and looked out the window. There was Friedrich, leaning against our car again. Obviously, he was assigned to me for the day. This time he was talking to a local Reinbeck motorcycle police officer and I wondered if my driver had violated some parking rule. He stood straight and pointed over his shoulder into my office window, unaware that I was looking out. The officer looked up and we made eye contact. He did not back away from my gaze and that caught me off guard. I guess it shouldn't have, cops don't back down. He looked back at Friedrich but didn't seem to say anything to indicate he saw me. Odd again. He then lifted his leg over the engine and sat astride his ride. He pushed the button for the electric ignition which started nearly silently, or so it seemed from my inside vantage point. He then looked back into the window at me, a slow deliberate look, as if he was trying to study my face. He adjusted his aviator sunglasses, nodded to Friedrich and rode away, no words of goodbye.

I headed out to talk with Friedrich, and nearly collided with Warner on his way back into my office. “The prosecutor will meet you for lunch in two hours. He will bring his investigator. But the meeting must be brief, only one hour.

The lunch will be at the Waldhaus Reinbeck at Loddenallee. Your driver knows it. It is a nice old building and they serve an excellent white asparagus and oxtail soup. It is also quiet at the rear table, away from the door and away from the kitchen. The prosecutor has already made the reservation." I wondered if Warner knew that was the hotel where I was staying?

"Thank you, Doctor. What about your team? When will your people be arriving? And my drawings?" I wanted to keep him busy, engaged, delivering my requirements and out of my way.

"The works-union manager should be here any moment. He lives closer than the others. We have almost all the drawings."

"Let's hold off on reviewing the drawings until I talk with the union boss. What is his name?"

"His name is Jürgen Jentzil. We all call him JJ."

"Yes," I replied. "I read that in his file. He has been with the company almost eighteen years. He has moved from labor representative to the head of the local works-union. I presume he has coordinated all that is going on here with his local management. Do you think this has reached the national union's attention yet?"

"Mein Gott, I hope not," Warner breathed.

I was convinced that if this got to the national level, we would have a harder time resolving it. It is hard to tell what leverage the national union would use to obtain their goals and objectives to the detriment of our plant interests.

“Let’s do all we can to keep this at the local level. What can I expect from Jürgen? What kind of resistance? And why would he not want to help the workforce get back to work? Is he in favor of protecting smugglers?”

“Smugglers? That is such an ugly word. We do not even know if there are any of our people involved.”

I could not believe the naivety of this presumed scholar. Why would the prosecutor take such drastic measures if all he had were mere allegations? His political career would be ruined if he was wrongfully heavy-handed, with no evidence to support him. And why would the works-union boss close ranks at the risk of fourteen hundred jobs? No, there was more here than just smoke. Somewhere a fire was burning. I needed to find out where and put it out, quickly. Warner was starting to ink his own name onto my suspect list.

Chapter Five

I WALKED OUT ONTO THE VERANDA AND motioned to Friedrich to come join me. He walked from the car and onto the porch. "What was that all about?" I asked.

He frowned as if he didn't understand. "What do you mean?" he asked.

"I saw you talking with a police officer. Is everything OK?"

"Oh, that. Yes, everything is fine. He saw the cars parked here and knew the plant was closed. He wondered if we were opening today."

"What did you tell him?"

"I told him the company had brought in their best investigator to help get the plant back open again."

"Best investigator, eh? What makes you think that?" I looked directly at Friedrich. I was curious how he got to that conclusion. I wanted to know who was talking to the driver of a third-party limo service, and I wanted to know why the motorcycle police officer seemed in charge of their conversation. I was looking at a red piece in a blue puzzle and trying to make it fit.

"I don't know why I said that," stammered Friedrich. "I knew you were a security person because they told me when I was assigned to drive you. I figured you were here to help re-open the plant. And I saw how the guard reacted when he saw your name."

"Why do you think a security person would have anything to do with the re-opening of the plant? Why not an engineer or a finance guy?" I sensed he knew more than he should have but didn't know who was talking to him.

"Doctor Warner told me that the company was sending you, a security person and I was to drive you wherever you wanted to go. He seemed angry that his boss would send an outsider from the U.S. to meddle with a local problem."

"Did he also tell you to report back to him on my movements, Friedrich?" I riveted him with a stare I reserved for when I moved in on a suspect in an interrogation. It was usually effective.

He glanced to his shoe tops and then

quickly back to me. “No sir. He did not say anything like that at all. He said to take you wherever you wanted to go.”

My eyes never left his, “Friedrich. It is OK. If I was Warner, I would tell you to keep an eye on me and to report back.”

He looked down again, examining his shoelaces a moment. It didn't take long to decide. “Yes. He did say he would like to be kept abreast of your activities. Please do not tell him I told you this. I could lose my job.”

“I tell you what, Friedrich, you say nothing but what I tell you to say to Warner. In return, I will say nothing to him about you coming clean with me.”

“Thank you. Thank you, sir. I will do as you say.”

I wasn’t so sure I could trust the guy but was going to work him regularly to test his adherence to our new agreement. And since I got that familiar tingle over the motorcycle cop, I was keeping Friedrich on a short leash too.

I nodded to him and walked back into the building. When Warner saw me walk in he said, “JJ will be here soon. I have only a large photo and some engineering drawings, but we can go over them until he arrives if you like.”

“No, come join me in my office first.” I replied. I wanted him to know that this was MY office now, especially after his decision to spy on me.

"Doctor Warner, I think it is only fair to tell you that I am unhappy with the way you have treated me and the way you have responded to my requests for help. I get the impression you have something to hide. I do not want to think it, but I am wondering if perhaps you are somehow involved in this problem." I saw his muscles involuntarily tighten in his jaw. I waited for his loud denial—the one that bursts forth from innocent people wrongly accused.

"I am not sure why you say that. What have I done?" he asked. No righteous, indignant outburst. Instead I got the all too familiar and involuntary response of someone who wants to know what you know before they answer your question.

"Doctor Warner, let's just say that I am keeping all my options open. And until you or I can establish that you are not somehow involved, you will be on my list. I still expect your complete and honest cooperation." Warner may not have driven a truck across the border, but I was thinking he was in possession of some kind of guilty knowledge. And it was only a matter of time before I found out. First, I had to show him that I knew what I was doing.

There was a knock on the door and the plant

engineer opened it cautiously. “Pardon me gentlemen,” he said. “JJ is here. Should I have him wait in my office?”

He had a generous office that could easily accommodate another person for a few minutes and I needed some more time to set the ground rules with Warner. “Yes,” I said. “Have him wait with you. We shall only be a few minutes. Feel free to tell him that you sense some tension in the office.” I looked directly at Warner as I said it. “Would that be an honest assumption on my part?”

The tense look on the Warner’s red face was all the confirmation he needed. “Yes, sir. I will let JJ know that we are all uncomfortable with the developments.”

“Perfect” I replied. And sent him out with a nod.

I motioned for Warner to sit, in the lower chair. He looked for another option but saw that I was intentionally seating him in the subordinate chair.

“Doctor Warner, here is the way this is going to go. I need to get this plant up and running again. I want the federal prosecutor to release it back into MY custody, for you to run until I leave. In order to make that happen, Felder is going to have to believe we are making progress in solving this case. He is going to want evidence of that progress in the form of your employees talking openly and honestly with me. The only way this is going to happen is for Jentzil, JJ, to give the word to the employees that it is okay to do so."

I could see that I lost him when I said the plant would be turned over to my custody. He hesitated. So, I went at it another way.

"Doctor Warner, Felder will want to hear us say that we are working with your team to gather records and we are trying to get the union to release the employees to talk. But more than that, he is going ask me if I believe you are stonewalling me. He will want to know if I think the union is blocking my investigation. So far, that is exactly what I think. Now what will you do to make me think otherwise?"

Warner looked at me, puzzled. He was already on record that he didn't like my presence. He already admitted that he was powerless against the union boss. He pretty much told Felder he was mistaken about company employees being involved in international smuggling. And he knew I didn't trust him.

"I do not know what you mean, Mr. Christian. If he already believes these things, what can I do or say to make him change his mind?"

"Well, Doctor, that is my question to you. How do you suggest we go about convincing Jentzil to cooperate?" I could tell he was not used to telling Jentzil what to do and that most differences of opinion were negotiated or settled in some quid pro quo. I was formulating a quid pro quo but hoping I would not have to use it.

"I will lead the conversation with Jentzil, Doctor Warner. When I look to you for back up or support, I expect you to deliver it. This is not open for debate. If I look to you and ask what you think, I am looking for you to enthusiastically agree, affirm and support my position. Can you promise me, right now, without knowing where I am coming from, that you will do this?"

He was silent a long time. I let him mull it over without interruption. Several times he looked down at his shoes. I wondered if it was a thing in Germany to regularly check the shine on your shoes.

Finally, he looked up. "Yes, I will do as you ask. You will have my support."

"And I do not want you to look like you are under pressure to agree with me, Doctor Warner. I want no backtracking and no softness in how you align yourself."

"Yes, I understand," he said.

"Good, then ask Leiter to bring in Jentzil."

Jürgen Jentzil walked with the air of a

confident man. A man used to confrontation and used to winning. But he was not at all like I pictured him. I was picturing a stocky, brush cut, thick neck – typical New York or Detroit union boss. Had it not been Germany, I would have expected a Bronx accent, a guy who was *connected* and who knew it. Not so with Jürgen Jentzil.

Jentzil was a medium sized guy in all respects. Not too heavy, maybe even lean. He wore dark blue khaki pants and a small-checkered button-down shirt – more engineer than union boss. He even had a pocket-protector – yes, a plastic pocket protector to go with his small chin and black-framed glasses. He did not look like a guy who would be double dealing the company. But as I had learned over two decades of investigating crimes and corporate corruption, looks didn't mean a damned thing.

It was also obvious he was pissed about coming in on a "day off." He acknowledged Warner with only a nod of his head, no polite greeting. He stood opposite me, on the other side of my desk, and waited for an introduction.

Warner helped with that. "JJ, this is Mr. Christian. He is the global head of security. Brinton has sent him here to fix our problem." This time he said it without the sneer in his voice. "We are to give him our complete cooperation. He speaks for Brinton and has total authority over the plant."

Jentzil looked directly at Warner, ignoring the courtesy of a greeting. "Oh, he does, does he? And does he have total authority over our workers as well? I do not believe that is within his purview. That is my responsibility and I do not relinquish it." He had yet to look at me or acknowledge my presence in the room.

Before Warner could respond, I cut in. "Doctor Warner, could you please excuse us?" I rose and walked to the door, opening it for Warner. His jaw began moving but no words came out. I looked him directly in the eyes reminding him of our agreement.

He nodded his head several times. "Of course, Mr. Christian. Of course." And he left the room. I could tell Jentzil was a bit taken aback by Warner's total capitulation.

As I returned to my desk, I pointed to the chair. "Sit down Mr. Jentzil." He stood there. "I prefer to stand," he said.

"Sit!" I barked. My bold abruptness caught him by surprise. Unsure, he eased himself into the chair, sinking into it. It was obvious he was not used to being addressed in this manner. Good.

I began what I had mentally rehearsed, "Mr.

Jentzil, we have …"

"Please, call me JJ," he said. "Everyone does."

"Mr. Jentzil," I continued. "I am not here as your friend, your family or new acquaintance. We have a very serious situation on our hands. It is a problem for which you share some responsibility. I am here to fix it and I will be needing your complete cooperation."

"Me? I have nothing to do with *the problem.*" He sneered. "Whatever problem exists is someone else's problem. Not mine. If you are going to *fix it,* then fix it. But do not involve me." He began to rise as if to leave.

"Sit and listen!" He did not object and eased himself back into the chair. I knew he would want to hear what I had to say, if for no other reason than to learn what I knew or what I proposed to do.

"The plant is closed. Our customers are not receiving their deliveries. Our suppliers want to be paid, but we are not generating any revenue. Our employees have no jobs. You claim to represent the workers of this plant, but as of now they are not drawing a paycheck. This is your doing." Jentzil visibly blanched when he heard that.

"I have nothing to do with the closing of the plant. This is the fault of the prosecutor. Felder is trying to make a name for himself and he is doing it at our expense. It is all over the news that the plant is idle during a government investigation."

I had not heard that before, but I should have figured as much. The situation took on an added dimension of importance. I would have to check with our public relations team in France to measure the impact. Whatever I did here was going to be somehow caught up into the media story about the plant closing. This could be high stakes for me as well. The look on Jentzil's face was again one of confidence. He had shifted the blame to someone else and was pleased with his telling of it.

I leaned in to Jentzil from across the desk. I wanted his attention and I wanted to create a sense of tension. "Listen to me Jentzil. Whatever you may have told your employees and whatever you may have told the national union, it is *you* who are responsible. And I have the power to make sure that everyone is aware that you closed the plant."

"That is not possible," he stammered. "I had nothing to do with it. Felder closed the plant."

"Felder closed the plant because you and Warner refused to cooperate. You instructed every employee to say nothing to Felder. He wishes to interview employees, but you have stood in the way and blocked all such efforts. I even have heard that you are advising your team that you will block my efforts to find out what is going on." I was fishing here, but his lack of denial confirmed my suspicions.

"Look here Jentzil. I am giving you one, and only one, chance. I have the authority to permanently close this facility. It has become a liability now. I can close it and someone else will oversee the selling of all its assets, and the packing and shipping of heavy equipment to another location. The company is already looking at other facilities in Germany and France if this plant stays idle any longer." He was listening and not blinking. I had him.

"If I do not hear soon from members of this workforce, with information about what is happening, I will make sure that every employee, and their sons and daughters and spouses know that it was your obstinacy that resulted in the plant being closed by the prosecutor. And I will make sure that the entire community knows that it was your decision to block the investigation that resulted in fourteen hundred workers being out of their jobs. And it will become known that our local suppliers, vendors and merchants had their businesses fall off, all because of you. I will make sure that the newspapers and television stations carry your story. And it will be personal. Not about the union, but about your bad judgment. You Jentzil. You will be portrayed as the cause of all that pain and suffering."

His pallor turned almost chalky.

"Or, I can portray you as a person who encouraged cooperation with the authorities and with the company's internal investigation. If that were to be the case, I am prepared to ensure that you are given interviews by the media and that we will help to shape a positive story for you. Of course, that offer is only good if you have nothing to do with illegal activity." I paused for dramatic effect.

"I want you to leave and think about this. I do not want you to ask your national union leaders for their opinion or for their direction. This is entirely on you." I saw his wedding ring. "Maybe you should talk with your wife about this. I will be back in three hours. I expect your decision at that time. I can assure you that if I do not receive your cooperation, this facility will close, and you will be shamed forever."

He looked so small sitting in that chair and I knew I had reached him. The key question remained, was he man enough to change his direction? And perhaps a bigger question was, did he have access to any information of value in solving this case? I supposed I would have to wait a few hours to learn the answer to both questions.

I stood. He pushed himself from the chair and walked with me toward the door without saying anything. I opened the door and whispered to him, "This may be the biggest decision of your life Jürgen. Don't blow it."

Warner stared at Jentzil as he left my office. I could tell he was looking for some sign from him about our conversation. The union boss left the building never looking up. "Doctor Warner please join me in my office and bring the prints."

As Warner gathered up the documents, I cleared his conference table and turned on the overhead light. "What do you want to look at first?" asked Warner. I could tell he was hoping I would let him in on the results of my conversation with Jentzil. He wasn't getting into my inner circle of confidants that easily.

"An aerial view," I replied.

Warner shuffled through some rolls of oversized paper and spread one out on the table. It was a large aerial photograph of the entire property. It seemed to have been taken about ten years prior. I asked him "Is this view current?"

"For an aerial view, it is the most current we have." Although it appeared to be no more than a large forest, a closer look revealed the outer road, the gated entrances to the facility, and corners of the administrative building and what turned out to be a machine shop. I looked it over briefly to get a sense of scale, compass orientation and its place in the overall neighborhood.

"Let me see a plot plan now." He rolled up the aerial plan and unfolded a large architectural rendering of the complex. He oriented it on the table in the same direction as had been the aerial view.

"This is the most current drawing we have that reflects our current buildings and structures. You can also see our perimeter fence line and the updated guardhouses."

"Please notice how the building layouts reflect our manufacturing process. Supply trucks enter through the northeast gates. Once they clear security, drivers are directed to a specific dock in the raw material storage building, there on your left. The driver is escorted to the truck drivers' lounge where he awaits the unloading of his vehicle. He is unable to enter the plant from the lounge. When unloading is completed, he is notified that he can leave with his truck. He leaves through the exit gate at the same guard office he entered."

I noticed that this was pretty much a standard receiving protocol. Nothing creative, but it still provided a few opportunities for abuse.

“Our production scheduler determines when to call for inventory from the raw material storage building. He was using his groomed index finger as a pointer, to demonstrate the process flow on the drawing. When the customer job number is created, the raw material warehouse supervisor is notified, and the parts are moved to the production facility, here. There they are placed on the line where they are assembled, machine stamped or forged into finished product. The job-completion paperwork accompanies them to the finished goods storage building next door.”

Again, I was not seeing anything creative. These were standard internal controls. But it was interesting to note that these buildings had been laid out in a production sequence since before World War II and it still performed well today.

"We have standing customer orders. These require us to ship certain goods to certain locations based upon predetermined customer requirements. Manifests are generated when the job is picked from the finished goods warehouse and prepared for shipment. Parts are counted and crated and affixed with their shipping document. Once crated, they are moved to a loading dock on this side of the building," he pointed to a wall of a building on the far side of the complex. It was an area not visible from the aerial photograph. "A third-party service is notified that we have a delivery and they dispatch a truck driver. Local deliveries, within a hundred miles, are handled by our own drivers."

I knew that it was at this point that the operation was most vulnerable and was very likely compromised. It was not possible to ship cargoes intrastate, interstate, or internationally without approved paperwork that would pass government inspection. When my team arrived this afternoon, we would immediately begin background checking key employees in the finished goods warehouse, the shipping department, and the loading department. Although it is very difficult to gather background information in Europe, it can be done. It just takes forever most times. Somehow, the drivers were involved. How they knew which loads to compromise remained to be seen.

"Doctor Warner, how many times a day do we ship internationally by road?"

"I do not have the details. But we have the paperwork outside that should give us the information. Would you like me to start going through it?"

"No. That will not be necessary. I have a

team coming that will be going through that information for me. Just separate it and make it available." Warner almost seemed disappointed. I had hoped he wanted to be part of the solution, but I was still a bit leery of giving him too much access to the direction of my investigation. The fact that I was honing-in on shipping was enough for him, for now.

"What time is my luncheon appointment, Doctor?"

"If you need a few minutes to freshen up, I would suggest you start now. Friedrich should be able to get you to the restaurant in about twenty minutes and your lunch is in about thirty minutes."

"Thank you I will do just that." I opened my briefcase, grabbed a couple extra business cards and my copy of my passport, the original of which was locked in the safe in my hotel. I placed them in my leather writing portfolio and locked my briefcase. "I will leave this in your office for safekeeping." And set it on the floor next to his desk.

Chapter Six

I FELT BETTER HAVING WASHED AND shaved my face. Although I had shaved earlier that morning, I felt I could use another and I was right. I felt refreshed and thought I appeared more energized. That was the impression I wanted to impart to Felder and Becker. Felder needed confidence that he could trust me, and Becker needed to believe I had the skills to deliver investigative support. A guy looking worn out and fatigued by lack of sleep would not convey that image.

Friedrich practically hopped off the fender of the Mercedes when he saw me exit the office. As he opened the rear passenger door, I tossed my portfolio into the car and slid across the seat, so I was behind him. He could not see me in the rear-view mirror.

"How long to the Waldhaus, Friedrich?"

"About 20 minutes, he replied. "I cannot go much faster. The rules here are very strict."

"Push the limit as far as you can. I want to arrive early."

"Yes," was his only reply as his foot tromped on the accelerator.

I met the maître 'de and asked for the reservation for Felder. He told me they had not yet arrived and walked me back to a table in the rear. It was indeed a quiet area, as promised. I took the only seat facing the door. I wanted a chance to assess these two before they saw me. And from my days as a cop I instinctively preferred facing the door.

Within minutes I saw two men in well-tailored suits enter, looking around to the rear. I could tell Felder right away. He carried himself as the boss. Becker was standing confidently, but slightly to his rear. The maître 'de pointed to the rear, indicating both the table and me.

As they approached, I rose. "Mr. Felder, Mr. Becker. Thank you for meeting me on such short notice."

"Yes," Felder perfunctorily replied. We shook hands and exchanged business cards.

"Please sit-down Mr. Christian. We have much to cover and only a little time. I have other appointments that I could not change." I sat, and they arranged their chairs facing more toward the front than they were originally positioned. Some instincts must be universal.

“So, Mr. Christian. I understand you have come a long way on very short notice from the States. The Concorde no less. Impressive. Doctor Warner says you are here to ‘fix this’ for me, whatever that means. Can you explain what that means?”

“Yes. Thank you. First of all, let me extend greetings on behalf of our Chief Executive Officer. I report directly to him and I have been put in full charge of the facility, although it is not functioning right now, as you know. Before I begin however, may I ask why you have shut down the plant? I imagine you have already received calls from our counsel in France and London. But I would like to hear it right from the horse’s mouth.”

“From the horse’s mouth, eh? It really is very simple Mr. Christian. I went to Doctor Warner seeking cooperation in my investigation, wherein unnamed employees of the plant were considered suspects in an International arms smuggling operation. Doctor Warner ---”

“Whoa! What? Arms smuggling? No one said anything to me about arms smuggling. Warner never mentioned a word about this to me, nor did our counsel.” I thought Felder and

Becker could tell by my reaction and the look on my face that I honestly didn't know.

"Well, we did not tell Warner or anyone else in your company about the weapons. We merely told him there was cause to believe employees were involved in smuggling."

I was still too stunned to let him go further without some explanation. "But weapons? How did we get from small time contraband to weapons?"

Becker and Felder looked at each other a long moment before Felder replied. "Let me just say that our people picked up a suspect in Rostock on unrelated charges. He was barely in custody when he began talking about making a deal in exchange for providing information on a smuggling operation. We thought he was talking about the cigarettes and tobacco case we were working out of your plant here in Reinbeck. Once he began talking we realized that his gun smuggling information and the contraband cases were possibly linked. Since we had no specific information about who may be involved from your company, we did not share everything with Warner. Surely, given your background you know how this works."

"My background? What do you mean?"

Felder smiled. "Mr. Christian. You are not playing with the boys in the alley. I am sure you have done your homework. We have too. Our friends at Interpol, Scotland Yard and even your FBI have vouched for both your integrity and your expertise. Why do you think we agreed to meet with you?"

"But how could you have done all that research? I have only been here a few hours?"

Again, Felder smiled smugly. "Our common friend Morgan called. He was looking for some assistance getting some 'resources' in place quickly and we confronted him about his client. While he did not reveal specifics, we were able to figure it out immediately. There is not much activity here in Reinbeck that would involve a call from Morgan. We had to bypass some rules. But your team will have no problem entering or being here this afternoon. As for your background check, it was easier than we thought. Your name came up in the Interpol files as having worked with England's Special Branch in Scotland Yard, both MI 5 and MI 6. It showed you broke a case for them involving Middle Eastern arms smugglers trading in gold in 1990. They were almost effusive about you, if a Brit can be effusive."

"And the FBI asked us to offer you any assistance you may need. Seems you helped them build the case against one of the conspirators in the 1993 World Trade Center

Bombing. They were surprised that you had not reached out to their office in Hamburg yet."

They had me with that last one. I usually check in with the State Department and the Bureau office when I arrive in any country outside the US. The Feds had a guy stationed here as well. But in my rush to get to the plant, I skipped that visit. I would have to remember to make that call as soon as I could today and hope that I hadn't bruised any egos.

"I am flattered that they mentioned anything and a bit disappointed to find myself in Interpol's databases." I replied.

Felder brushed it off. "Here is the deal, Mr. Christian. We seized the plant because this is an important case and your people stonewalled us. We figured the smuggling operation could not continue if we shut it down. It might even force them to make a mistake. Our terms for re-opening it are simple. Provide the persons responsible. Lacking that we want access to possible employee witnesses and your company paperwork and we will open the plant. It is all we asked for from the beginning."

Felder's explanation was as simple as it was superficial, and it certainly wasn't good enough to help me get the plant re-opened. They had given me nothing to help me break this case in any reasonable period of time. I could almost hear the money falling through the cracks in the factory floor as we wasted these minutes posturing over lunch.

"Let me ask you a question Mr. Felder. You seem to know what you are doing. Why haven't your people conducted a surveillance? Wouldn't that be easier?"

It was Becker who replied. "That option was taken off the table when we decided to close the plant. Nothing could move cross-border and so it made no sense. As important as this case is, we have limited resources without solid suspect information." I read something else into it and my thoughts were confirmed when I saw a glance pass between Felder and Becker.

Felder interrupted Becker. "Mr. Christian, we did run a surveillance and a very costly one. It produced nothing of value in the way of suspects. We ultimately had to return the staff resources we borrowed from other agencies."

"So," I offered, "It would have made more sense to keep the plant open and run a surveillance on outbound vehicles heading for border crossings. But because of Wagner's reluctance you pulled the trigger too quickly. Now you are living with a stalemate."

"Perhaps, it can be construed that way, Mr. Christian, but we prefer to characterize it as having tapped out our leads and run out of resources. We thought we could make up that ground and get reauthorized for surveillance crews when we built a better case with the help of your management team. But when Warner and Jentzil blocked that avenue, we decided to show them we were very serious about resolving this. We were not going to go away."

I saw an opening. "Let me make a proposal. I speak for the company, so I need no one's permission. I will get you the documentation you need, by close of business, in two days or less. Operations, shipping, whatever you need. My investigation results will be yours and I will do everything in my power to get you access to witnesses of fact by the same time. As you know, I am bringing in private resources of the highest caliber and we will conduct an internal investigation. I give you my word, that as soon as we have actionable evidence, we will turn it over to you."

"And in exchange?" Ever the attorney, Felder asked the key question.

"And in exchange, I would like permission to re-open the plant tomorrow morning on the day shift. It will be a light shift, mostly engineers, maintenance and boiler operators to get the plant re-started. I further promise you that if I cannot get full cooperation from the union and Doctor Warner, you can re-close the plant. But I warn you, if you do that, I will shutter the plant permanently. I will not see our assets, company goodwill and our financial loss used as a bargaining chip. And that will put fourteen hundred of your citizens out of a job. I have that authority, but I absolutely do not want to use it. Gentlemen, we both have a lot at stake here. We both want to succeed, not to close a plant. Let us work together and see what happens."

Felder was taking it all in. I could see it was a lot to digest. But I could see he liked the bait. The only question was would he run with it and let me set the hook?

"Mr. Christian. Although you come well recommended, you are asking me to go back to my superiors and tell them that I have changed my mind. That an American has come over here and strong-armed me or made happy-talk with me and convinced me to release the only leverage we have. That is a bit much for me to agree to."

I knew this wasn't going to be easy, but I had more to offer. "Herr Felder, a moment ago you mentioned that you had tapped out your resources and that the investigation had ground to a halt. Keeping the plant closed will not produce any change in the investigation. In fact, it will eventually lead to a media frenzy as they latch on to stories of family hardship caused by the plant closing. And they will certainly use the financial losses and downstream customer plant closings and layoffs as fodder for follow-up coverage.

"You certainly realize that one way to get the suspects active again is to re-open the plant. But I am also thinking it would be giving them a license to continue, if we do not have a plan to intercept and disrupt them. Please sir, allow me the opportunity to serve in the capacity of disrupter. I have excellent resources, no disrespect to Herr Becker and your team. I have the capability to mount fixed and moving surveillances. I now own the plant operations and will soon have gathered up the necessary documents that you asked for. And I believe I can manage the head of the works union into paving the way for employee interviews. Please Herr Felder, give this some serious consideration. I give you my word, I will work tirelessly to help you bring this to a conclusion."

Felder had been listening intently. His body language was cautious, but not hostile. I thought he was being fair in his consideration. At least that is what I was hoping.

Felder stood and so did Becker. "Could you excuse us for just a few minutes, Mr. Christian? I would like to talk privately with Obermeister Becker. When we return, we may have lunch, or not. Just a few minutes. Thank you." With that, he left the table and walked to the front of the restaurant.

I rose and walked to the bar. So, Morgan had called Felder. Morgan never needed permission for his guys to cross a border. They just did, using whatever passport they needed. Morgan probably suspected that if Felder inferred he was helping me, Felder would be more comfortable with me.

Brilliant. This is why I never ask Morgan what anything costs. He had greased the skids and never mentioned it. And it seemed that I had left Scotland Yard and the Feds in London and New Jersey in good standing, given the nice references I had received. But I really was a bit disturbed to be in the Interpol files. Not all the participants of Interpol were on my list of trustworthy countries. But there was nothing I could do about that.

I ordered a Crown Royal on the rocks. They had the Canadian brand on the shelf, which impressed me, given Reinbeck was not a major metropolitan German city frequented by US or Canadian businessmen. I enjoyed the way the first sip warmed as it went down and left no bitter burn on my tongue. This would either calm me or put me to sleep. There was a lot riding on the next few minutes.

Looking in the bar mirror, I could see Becker and Felder in animated discussion. Abruptly, Felder raised his hand to conclude the talk and rose from the table. He walked to the maître 'de stand and shortly he was dialing the house phone. After only a few minutes, he walked back to our table. Seeing me watching, he motioned for me to follow from the bar.

"Mr. Becker and I have talked over your proposal. We have discussed it with my superiors. I must tell you I did not get a warm response from the Chief Prosecutor. He asked why we were surrendering the plant without anything positive in the way of new and incriminating evidence. I mentioned your background, your past experiences on major cases and the favorable review from other agencies. He was not as impressed as I was. In fact, he made it my choice. But he put the consequences of failure quite bluntly to me Mr. Christian. This is a career breaker. If this goes poorly, or if we do not properly resolve the case, I am likely going to be in this position for the rest of my career. It is not my intention to remain at this level. This is a very high-risk scenario that you propose. For your company, there is a lot at risk if the plant remains closed. For your customers, there is much concern about their own productivity. And for me personally, this could be the end."

"However, I have recommended your offer and they have accepted. I do not know you Mr. Christian, but I believe in your honesty, and your track record speaks to your ability to get results. So yes, we will return your plant. But I have one firm condition. I am assigning Obermeister Becker to your investigation team, imbedded if you will. He will be my eyes and he may prove a valuable asset to you. He has total and nearly encyclopedic knowledge of this case and of the area. But I must warn you, if he believes for one moment that you are, how do you say, '*merely paying us lip-service*,' or just spinning your wheels in order to get your plant back, we will close it. This is not negotiable."

I knew I was not in a negotiating position and this was a win-win for both of us, whether he thought so yet or not. I was also secretly thrilled to add Becker to the team, even though he would be reporting our every movement to Felder. I was hoping we could overwhelm him with energetic progress. Hopefully this was all good news.

"I accept your terms Herr Felder. Please accept my thanks and convey my sincere gratitude to your superiors." Although I was too excited for a meal, I asked "Shall we eat? I understand the oxtail soup is delicious."

We must have all been too excited. We each only got the soup and some crusty bread. As we dipped the Bauernbrot into the broth and ate, we tried to make light conversation and to bond socially, but we all felt the fear of failure taking the enjoyment from the moment. We were done in less than an hour, and as I paid the bill, Becker came over and mentioned he would join me at the office, where I was now officially setting up a command post. I liked that about him. He would be by in less than an hour. I swear, I thought he had a gleam in his eye that almost looked like enthusiasm to be back in the chase.

Friedrich drove me back to the plant in record time.

▪ ▪ ▪ ▪ ▪

I wasn't ready to let Warner know yet that I had struck a deal with Felder. But when Becker arrived, Warner would know something was up. I had a half hour or so to prepare and I needed Warner completely on board. I thought about the best way to maximize the impact of the good news. Warner needed to know that I was the real McCoy and was capable, far beyond his abilities, to bring this problem to closure.

"Doctor Warner, your Federal Investigators may have blinked. They have turned the plant back over to me on a limited basis."

Warner was stunned. The look on his face was precious. "How did you? What did they? I mean this happened so fast. How did you get them to free the plant?"

"It is quite simple Doctor Warner. I am giving them what they are asking for. First, they demanded that Investigator Becker be assigned to my team. He should be arriving soon. Secondly, I assured them that whatever I discovered, I would forward to Felder. I promised him that I would have witnesses for him, factual witnesses who have something to contribute to the investigation."

Warner interrupted me. "You have witnesses? Already? You have someone who saw an employee stealing? How can that be? You just arrived? Who are they? I mean who are the witnesses or who are the thieves? Has JJ released the employees to talk with you? He never said a word to me about it." The good Doctor seemed uncomfortable in his own skin. I couldn't tell if it was because he was guilty, had guilty knowledge, or was just overwhelmed to think that the allegations could actually be true. His world was spinning out of control and he was unaccustomed to not being in charge – especially of his own destiny. I let his confusion take full effect before I responded.

"Slow down, Doctor. No, I do not have witnesses – not yet. But I will. And yes, Jentzil will allow the employees to talk with me. He will actually provide me a list of people to talk with. He should be calling any minute, asking to see me." I was bluffing on this one but had that gut feeling Jentzil was going to cooperate.

Warner seemed doubtful. "You do not know JJ, Mr. Christian. He is stubborn, and he keeps his job in the union by protecting his people, not by betraying them. And besides, I have no reason to believe JJ knows what is going on or who is involved. Frankly, I have no reason to believe anything is going on at all. We have only the prosecutor's word on this and he is a political person, wanting higher office."

"Let me ask you a question Doctor. You are a reasonable and educated man. Do you honestly believe that Felder would close a plant this size on a whim or a hunch? If he guessed wrong, or lacked credible evidence, what do you think would happen to his political aspirations? What would happen to his career? No, he is not guessing. I have spoken with him. I can assure you that he has more than mere speculation to go on. He believes he is very close to solving this case, but only with our help.

"So, here is the deal. JJ will see me today. My team will be here shortly. I do not want JJ to know, under any circumstances, that the plant has been released to my custody. I will tell him when I am ready. Do you understand what I am saying Doctor Warner? I want no misunderstanding. No one is to know until I tell them or until I give you specific information to share, not even your wife. Now repeat what I have told you."

I could tell he resented being told what to do and resented being treated like a child. But I didn't care. I had a point to make. And if he breached my confidence, I wanted to be able to fire him on the spot as an example to everyone else.

"I am to tell no one without your permission."

"Tell them what?" I pushed.

"Anything. I am to tell no one anything, even my wife, without your permission."

"Yes," I replied, "Not even your secretary."

"Yes, not even her."

"Okay Doctor, you can tell I am dead serious about this. Do not worry about plant start up crews or anything else of that nature until I tell you. Now explain to me what inventory was left on the docks awaiting delivery when the plant was closed."

Warner said he had to get some shippers and would be right back. I held the door open for him as he exited and left it open, so I could see in the general bullpen area. He walked into the customer order entry area and I could see him sifting through papers on someone's desk. He grabbed a small stack and returned.

"These were crated and labeled, and they might still be on the docks. I do not know which got onto the trucks before the police seized the plant." He showed me several shipping manifests and bills of lading.

"It would have been less than a truckload," I noted.

"Yes. That is correct. But these are to customers in different regions and represent three different truck routes." I knew which directions I was interested in but did not single any one out for him.

"Where would the trucks be headed?" I asked.

"This small load is going to Basel, Switzerland, the Monteverdi luxury car manufacturer. The delivery is mostly assembled electronics, wiring packages, harnesses, and in–dash equipment. We do not normally do full assembly OEM unless by special order. But for them, we have a standing order." I knew my interests were not with a Monteverdi shipment. It was heading in the wrong direction.

"And the next one?" I asked.

"This shipment was going to Poland. The

parts would be delivered to multiple locations for the Chevy Aveo, The Opal Astra III and IV, and the Fiat 500. Let me see… No, not on this load. We normally also ship for the Fiat 500 and the Fiat Panda but there are no such parts on this shipper. It is also a partial load and not a full truck. Hmmmm."

Poland was my direction of interest—east. "What is odd about that one Doctor? Why the hesitation?"

"Well, we normally try to put together a full load to Poland because next to Germany, they are the largest, geographically-local, manufacturer of automobiles. At least local to our plant here in Reinbeck. Great Britain, France and Italy are larger, but they are farther from us."

"Doctor," I interrupted. "What is odd about this shipper?"

"As I mentioned, we normally try to fill a truck rather than sending a partial load. It makes better sense to us and our customers if we keep the shipping costs down. Lately, there have been several less than full truckload deliveries to Poland. It is almost as if production scheduling is less coordinated in that direction. We actually had a team scheduled to study it just before the plant closed. I am sure our quality people will start again as soon as we return."

I was familiar with the less than truckload concept and understood supply chain logic. This might be the tip I had been waiting for.

"Tell me about the other shippers, Doctor." I wasn't really interested beyond the Polish delivery. But didn't want to telegraph my eagerness to focus on it.

As he droned on, I began shaping the direction I would have my team working.

Warner was interrupted by the phone ringing. "That is my phone ..." He looked at the desk I was occupying and then at me.

"I will get." I replied. He stood there, so I nodded to the door.

It was Jürgen Jentzil. I took the call.

"Mr. Christian. I have been thinking about what you said. Let us assume for the moment that I was willing to let the people talk with you."

"Only the people with something to offer, Jürgen."

"Yes, that is my point. If I only allow people with something important to offer, they will each be identified as, how do you say it, *snitches*?"

"Yes, that is how we say it. And I see your point."

"No, there is more. If I produce people with something to contribute, then it will be presumed that I knew what was going on or may have been involved. The prosecutor may want to charge me too, for not coming forth. I am in a delicate position here, Mr. Christian."

There was a side of me that saw his dilemma right away. I had seen it before. There was a side of me also that wanted to put the screws to Jentzil for allowing fourteen hundred workers to go without their paychecks for a week already. Whether he had something to hide or not, I had to get past him and to the witnesses.

"I know you do not know me Jürgen, but I have standing with the prosecutor. Maybe there is something we can do. But first you must know this. If you are involved, you will have to cut a deal with the prosecutor on your own. If you help me here, I will promise to put in a good word for you. Perhaps, depending on what you know, I may be able to convince him that you came forth willingly with information before any of the others. It is the best I can do."

"But you should also know Jürgen, if you do not cooperate with me, I will close the plant. And it will not be just the fourteen hundred employees that want to know why. It will be their families, and those of all the suppliers and customers who also got screwed by your hesitancy. Are we clear on that?"

There was silence on the other end of the phone – a long silence. When he spoke, I could barely hear him, “Yes. I have spoken with my wife about this. It was as if the two of you had talked. Or if not, she has an amazing ability to see things the way you do. I am *ferplutched* no matter what I do or not. She suggests, and I have come to agree, that it is best for everyone if I cooperate. I will be in your office in ten minutes. I am close by.”

I did not know what “ferplutched” meant, but my guess was close enough. He was indeed screwed no matter what. I answered, “I will see you then.” And hung up.

I wasn’t sure how Jentzil could have intimate knowledge of participants without being involved. But I knew that I would figure it out soon enough.

The afternoon was getting clogged with appointments. I hoped I could manage them without wasting anyone’s time or missing something important.

“Doctor Warner,” I called out. “Please arrange for several boxes of sweet pastries, some cheeses, breads and fruits, and lots of coffee and bottled water. This is going to be a long night.”

▪ ▪ ▪ ▪ ▪

Jentzil arrived within minutes and now stood in my office doorway. “Sit down,” I offered. “Do you want a water or a coffee? Doctor Warner is rounding up some things for us." I wanted to make him somewhat comfortable. Not to diminish the gravity of the situation, but to make him at ease with what was going to be self-incriminating no matter how we tried to smooth it over.

"No, I am fine," he said. "First, I want to thank you for pushing me to this decision. I have been struggling with this for a long time."

I did not acknowledge his thanks. "Jürgen, before we go any farther, I want to tell you that I am not a policeman. I am not a private investigator. And I do not work for the prosecutor. What I am trying to do here is to get these people, your friends and co-workers, back to work and earning their paychecks. Our company wants this plant back operating. The prosecutor thinks that by squeezing the workers the company will capitulate. He is likely right about that, but it does not mean we are in a bad bargaining position. As the community waits this out, they are beginning to turn against the prosecutor for hurting the workers, but you and I know the truth. We know that Felder did not intend to close the plant. But when you refused to allow the workers to talk with him, or me for that matter, he was backed into a corner. So, he shut the plant. Basically, YOU shut the plant.

The neighbors here haven't figured that out yet."

I paused to let that sink in before I continued. "Now, having said that, I believe we are at a moment of opportunity where everyone wins. You too. So, let's start at the beginning. Who will be talking with me, and what do they have to offer? Let us start with you JJ, what is it that you want to get off your chest?"

"As I said, Mr. Christian, I really do not have any involvement. But perhaps I can offer some insight. Let me start with what I know for fact and then we can move to who may be willing to talk with you. A few months ago, about eight months actually, I …"

The door to my office opened unexpectedly. "Excuse me for interrupting, Mr. Christian, but your team is here." I am sure Warner could tell from the look on my face, that his disruption could not have come at a worse time. Jentzil would not turn around in his chair. He obviously did not want to make eye contact with Warner, whose attention was riveted on the back of Jentzil's head and not on me.

"Doctor Warner, next time I have someone in my office, remain outside. Do not enter without permission and do not disturb me. You know the number to this room. Do not knock, just dial the number. If I pick up, fine. If not, then just wait. I do not care who is outside. Do you understand? Do I make myself perfectly clear?"

"Yes, Mr. Christian. My apologies. What should I tell your team?" He still was not looking at me when he answered. It was as if he was trying to get inside Jentzil's head by boring a hole in it with his eyes.

"Tell them I am in an interview. They will understand. Give them some pastries, make them comfortable and see to their needs for any supplies they may want. Thank you. You may go now." I dismissed him with cold regard. I wanted Jentzil to see that I was dominating the relationship and that he had nothing to fear from Warner.

"Mr. Christian. I have been thinking. Perhaps I do not know anything of value. I want to help, of course. But I am just a worker here as well. I only do my job and try to help my union brothers. I stay out of the way."

Just as I figured. The mood was broken. Warner had succeeded, if that was what he was trying to do, in stopping my forward movement. Well, I had seen cold feet creep in before and I knew how to warm them up again. Not my favorite ploy, but I could hold Jentzil's feet to the fire equally well.

"JJ, let me take a step back with you. I know your wife thinks you are now doing the right thing, whatever she thinks that is. You know that fourteen hundred of your brothers want to come back to work. Right now, they believe either what you have told them, or what they think they know—that a handful of fellow workers are up to "mischief" and that the entire might of the government, *Großer Bruder*, Big Brother, is trying to put them in jail for minor offenses. You may even believe that to be the case."

"But I have been around a long time doing this Jürgen. And I think you know this as well. The prosecutor is going after something really big here, not some simple act of smuggling cigarettes or liquor. Something really important, or he would not be closing an entire plant.

"Do you understand Jürgen? Can you imagine how significant this must be for him to go to these extremes? Do you know how many government officials had to sign off on a plant closing of this magnitude?"

I watched him taking this all in. He was leaning forward – elbows on his knees and his head down. The weight of it was pushing on his shoulders so heavily he could barely sit upright. He may not have had all the details of what was going on, but he knew who was involved. Knew at least some of the players. That information was what I needed. And I needed it before tomorrow. I needed to snap him out of it before he got too low.

"Jürgen!" I shouted. I am sure they heard me outside the door.

Once I was sure I had his undivided attention and he had regained his composure, I continued quietly. "Do you hear me, Jürgen? Your opportunity to stay uninvolved is over. I can see to it that you are known either as a help to the investigation, which may save your job and reputation, or that you blocked it when you had a chance to be helpful, which may send you to prison. Either way, the call is yours. But I assure you, you will not have another chance to go home and make up your mind. Now sit up and start at the beginning."

He did not sit up. I could barely hear him. It was as if his lungs did not have enough air to push the words out through his lips. "I should have known there was more to it than I was being told. You are right. I have been a fool. I had no idea that damned prosecutor would close the plant. Once he did, there was no backtracking for me. And Warner was fit to be tied. He insisted we close ranks and prove the prosecutor a fool. Warner was talking about ruining that *niedrig günstling*, that lowly minion, as he calls Felder. It became a vendetta between Warner and the prosecutor. I am glad you are here Mr. Christian. It is time to end this. We are all worried sick. It has been going on for longer than the polizei know."

He started right in, without any additional prompting from me. "I do not know anything for sure, Mr. Christian and I have seen nothing first hand. But I have been in conversations where I have heard that someone is driving cigarettes and liquor into Poland, perhaps more than just one of our drivers. I have heard that there may be some relatives outside the company who are part of this too. But production does not seem to be affected. No one is late with deliveries. I have heard that there have been some unusual routes given to some drivers, however management does not seem to think it is important enough to look into. Given our exceptional operational quality, we have not seen the value in disrupting the workplace by forcing the issue."

It was obvious that Jentzil also still did not see where the connection was between the smuggling operation and the plant closing.

He continued, "Given what I have heard is going on and from what I am able to put together on my own, I believe you will find some merit in talking with a handful of people first. I mean the people who control our orders, people on the dock and in shipping. I will call them and ask them to talk with you."

I already knew where to start my

investigation. His contribution, so far, had been only the obvious.

"Jürgen, I am wanting more of you. I want you to tell me what you have heard, and who it was that said it. I want to know who was present at those conversations, whether they seemed to be actively involved or were just a bystander to a conversation. I want to know when those conversations occurred and where they took place. And to the extent you know, or have strong suspicions, I want to know who is involved in this. This is not a matter of you unjustly accusing anyone. This is a matter of me ruling out anyone who may be under suspicion. When I am through, those falsely suspected will be exonerated and those responsible we be discovered. This is about details Jürgen. I am not just having a polite talk with you. This is an investigation. But before we begin, can I offer you a coffee or some water?"

Jentzil declined, saying he wanted to begin right away. It was almost as if he couldn't wait to get *it* off his chest. Whatever "it" was. He began talking as if his story was forcing itself out of him.

Chapter Seven

TOBIAZ WAS EXHAUSTED, WHICH ONLY added to his frustration. He dreaded that he was having another meeting with Anatoly. The cold skies had opened into a light rain and as the temperatures dropped, black ice had formed over several patches of the road from Szscecin to Rostock. Several times during the last half hour, he had to reduce the speed. The ride should only have taken two hours, but it seemed to take forever. Anatoly's earlier arguments with Ulrich and Tadeusz in Rostock were worrisome, and that further wore him out. When Anatoly pulled the gun on Ulrich, he was terrified. He was sure at the time that Anatoly was going to kill Ulrich. Frankly, he was becoming more and more frightened and that drained him the most. He could not wait to get with Karol. He no longer felt it was worth continuing. Let the Russians figure out their own connections. The extra cash was nice, but this level of fear was so much more than he had bargained for.

To some degree, Tobiaz always worried about being detained, but after all this time, that aspect bothered him less and less. If Customs officers searched their loads, he could always plead ignorance of the contents. They had the shipping papers authorizing the deliveries of the closed crates. They were just company truck drivers as far as anyone was concerned. No, that wasn't what frightened him. It was this damned association with the Russians. And it would not be easily explained to a Customs agent if they were challenged.

Tobiaz worried for so many reasons. It would mean hell to pay if they were caught together and it would make explaining too difficult. Both their warehouses were not on Tadeusz's original delivery routes and this made Tadeusz uneasy to the point of wanting to quit. Ulrich had begged off the last delivery by feigning illness at work.

Tobiaz was also fraught with a deeper misgiving—the fact that these guys were armed. He felt that if a Customs agent got too suspicious, Anatoly or Gennady wouldn't hesitate to shoot. No, it was time to get out before someone got hurt and they became involved in a murder.

Snow clouds were forming high up, while a thick, frosty mist formed at ground level—not quite a fog. The black, moonless sky deepened the already dark shadows and sucked the illumination from his headlights that barely lit the route. When he finally arrived, he was exhausted. Tobiaz pulled the truck to the dock and ran up the stairs to the pedestrian door. It was locked. Odd. Karol should have been in there waiting for him.

He pounded on the steel door twice with his fist and it opened from inside. Tobiaz could see Gennady's form outlined in the doorway. He couldn't see Karol's truck and it worried him. There was no other truck in the yard. Where was Gennady and Anatoly's truck if they were here already?

Above the steady pelting of sleet, Tobiaz could hear the overhead door chains rattle as the door began rising. The cold raced right through his coat collar. At the rear of the truck, he unlocked the padlock on the double doors and opened each, folding them back along the side panels. He jumped back into the warmth of the truck and looked into his rearview mirrors. Although Tobiaz was an expert truck driver, he could barely see the dock in the faint light. He thought to himself that he should have stayed on his routes as a short haul driver, working out of the union hall. But the allure of all this extra cash made it difficult to be available as an on-call driver. He eased the gear into reverse adeptly and backed to the dock sill. As he shifted the gear into first and turned off the engine, he could hear sound of a diesel forklift starting. Before Tobiaz even got out of the truck, Gennady had already slipped the forks under their crate and was backing it into the warehouse. And by the time he got to the bottom of the steps, Anatoly was lowering the overhead door. Still no sign of his brother.

The concrete floor of the warehouse was as frigid as the frozen dirt outside, maybe colder. Tobiaz could feel it through the lug soles of his boots. There was no warmth at all in the building. Two high intensity work lights had been set up on tripods and they seemed to be giving off the only heat in the place.

"Where is Karol?" Other than Gennady and Anatoly, the warehouse seemed empty.

"He is not here." Blunt, but not answering the question, Anatoly seemed to dare Tobiaz to press the issue. So, he did.

"Where is he? Where is Karol? How did you get in here?" Ignoring the Pole, Gennady muttered something in Russian, a guttural dialect that Tobiaz could not place.

"Anatoly, what did he say? Where is my brother?"

Both the Russians were glaring at Tobiaz, as if to make a point about being disturbed. Tobiaz could barely see their faces, but the look felt menacing.

"He left in his truck and said he will meet you at your warehouse in Szczecin. He did not want to wait with Gennady. Gennady says, 'good riddance.' Now that our crate is here and yours is on your truck, you can go. I will call you about next load. Next time we introduce Gennady to your cousins. In case something happens to a driver."

Tobiaz was outraged. This was his warehouse, not the Russians. And how the fuck did they get in here? And where was his brother? It all seemed like bullshit to Tobiaz.

He was about to push it further when Anatoly said, "We will be out of here soon. We need only to look into our crate to make sure. Then we will leave. And no, we did not break in. Your brother agreed to let us in to wait for you. Then he decided not to wait here with us. He said he would meet you at your home."

Tobiaz sensed something terribly wrong with the explanation. It made no sense, but Anatoly left no room for further questions. There was nothing to gain by pressing this with the Russians, except a bullet. He had to get back to Szczecin and talk with Karol. Their warehouse and their routes were compromised. This was the end if Tadeusz's role at the plant became compromised.

He could see this was not the time, place or company for further discussion or polite goodbyes. He turned to walk out the door but stopped for one last look at these two new "partners." They had already turned their backs to him and were prying the lid off the crate. This was his chance to see what was inside, if for no other reason than to confirm his suspicions. He leaned into the darkness of a pillar. The frozen concrete chilled him to his bones.

Anatoly must have heard his footsteps stop. He turned his head slightly but did not look back. "You know what is saying about curiosity and cat. You do not want to know what is in crate. Go home."

Tobiaz backed to the door and left. He turned the heater on full blast when he got in the truck. His hands and feet felt like ice and his whole body shivered violently. He pulled the truck almost to the outer gate before stopping to close its rear doors. He couldn't stand to be near those two any longer. Once he got this truck unloaded in Szczecin, it would be his last delivery. He and Karol had to get out of this mess.

He cracked the window a bit to air out the truck and accelerated onto Ulmenstrase then headed south out of Rostock. That would get him onto Autobahn 19 and toward his eastbound connection on Autobahn 20. He did not want to be any later than he already was getting to Karol. Unfortunately for them both, he was already was too late.

Chapter Eight

TYLER ANDERSON WAS THE FIRST TO arrive in Hamburg. He cleared the Bundespolizei inspection station without issue and proceeded directly to the Europcar rental office inside Terminal One. He picked up his keys and paperwork and then crossed the footbridge to the parking structure where the rental cars were parked. Arrangements had been made for him to drive a Mercedes 560 SEL because it had extra room in the cabin and a larger trunk for gear. He looked in the back to make sure he had the right one. He loaded his personal duffle into the trunk, next to the other black leather bags already there. He then drove back to the outer loop of the airport and headed for passenger pickup at Terminal Two, where he would pick up his two partners on this assignment.

Tyler loved this kind of work. He actually enjoyed being called without any foreknowledge of an event and being asked if he was available at a moment's notice. He was single, and he had a great deal of freedom to come and go as he pleased from his job in London. He could hardly call it work. His assignment at the State Department was pretty much unsupervised, except out of Virginia. He came from a unit known for its deployment to unconventional warfare engagements and other "special assignments." It allowed him to be creative without too many people second-guessing the decisions he made in the field. At least not at the time they were being made. That freedom allowed him time to make a few extra dollars on the side – very good dollars. And he liked being on-call to Morgan Andercott.

Morgan was not miserly when it came to compensation and he never questioned Tyler's invoice for time or expenses, especially since he knew that his expenses were being passed along to the clients. Morgan left him to problem solve as he saw fit, so he was again pretty much unsupervised. Corporate crimes were so much easier to resolve and rarely involved bloodshed, at least for the most part. It didn't mean he didn't prepare, but the risks were a lot lower than his previous work as a Special Forces Officer.

When Tyler got the call, he personally hand picked his crew with Morgan. Guys he not only knew and had worked with before, but who possessed the skills and temperament to transition to the corporate arena. Not everyone could make that adjustment from operative to investigator.

The first member of Tyler's team, Peter Martin, would be arriving from Paris shortly. His flight was cheap and fast, and he would have only his carry on duffle. The third member, Kent Green, was already stationed in Germany, Hamburg to be specific. The guys traveled light taking only what they needed to get them through the next several days, if necessary. Anything else they may need was already in the Mercedes.

Kent had taken a taxi to the airport. As he paid the driver, he looked up and saw Peter coming out of the doors for passenger pickup. "Hey Peter, good to see you again. It's been too long brother."

Peter looked up from his notes. "Kent!" He smiled warmly and gave his friend a hearty handshake. "Way too long. I think last time was ..." He paused, remembering.

"Yes, it was at Randy's funeral."

It had been two years but seemed just a

short while ago when they buried a friend who was part of their team.

Kent, Peter, Tyler and Randy had been part of a combined Kuwaiti, British and US Special Forces unconventional warfare team in Operation Desert Storm. Their knowledge of the country, the language and customs, and their post-war connections put them back together again in Afghanistan a few years later.

A battle-hardened team of Yanks and Brits was dropped in-country on a mission to bring out Kamal El Hani, a member of the al-Qaeda Islamic Jihad group and one of the money men behind the World Trade Center bombing of '93. The goal was to get him out alive, grab any documentation they found, and squeeze all the intelligence they could from him until he was no longer of any value. A very well-paid drug dealer identified that El Hani was hiding out with a contingent of jihadists in the small town of Mehter Lam about two hours east of Kabul, Afghanistan.

By plan, they entered the house at four o'clock in the morning while El Hani slept with his wife in their small alshaalih. Quickly and silently, as they had rehearsed, they captured El Hani without firing a shot. But the plan did not call for them to take the wife. So, she was overpowered and left behind, gagged and tied to a chair. Using her shoulder though, she soon loosened her gag and let out a terrible wail.

Rallying gunmen from the household opened fire on their group as they fled into the yard with El Hani. Randy returned fire to provide cover while the team got El Hani inside their armored personnel carrier. With their prisoner secured, they called for Randy to retreat as well. But before he could even turn to jump into the already rolling APC, he was gunned down. The team unleashed awesome firepower on the tribal fighters as Kent leapt back into the yard and retrieved Randy's already dead body into the vehicle. The somber group drove on to their extraction point and out of the country with El Hani.

Their mission was by all other accounts a success. But no one on the team could muster any satisfaction from losing their British brother. Although no one said it was due to Randy's death, their group was broken up shortly after they were extracted from their forward base in Saudi Arabia. Randy's body was flown home to London.

Kent and Peter looked at each other, oblivious to the cars driving by the curb. A honking horn broke their reverie. It was Tyler, the third member of their Ops team. He popped the trunk and ran to the curb, giving each friend a bro hug. His smile was contagious. These were fast friends whose bonds were forged in the fire of combat.

Communications, technology, investigations, German customs and language were the special skills Morgan assembled for this engagement and this was the team. Tyler tossed Kent the keys. "You drive. You know the area. Toss your gear in back boys and we'll be on our way. I've got some Brotchen rolls, fresh meats and some iced Becks and Warsteiner's in a cooler back there. We can eat, talk and drive. I'll fill you in with what little I know. We'll be at the plant in less than an hour."

■ ■ ■ ■ ■

Warner was not at ease with these three new men who walked into his plant like they owned it. Once they realized he wasn't Michael Christian, they seemed to pay no attention to his status. As soon as he advised them that Mr. Christian was in an interview, they seemed to take it in stride that they would have to wait until he was finished to meet with him.

Warner wasn't in the mood for entertaining them either. After they introduced themselves to Warner, he pointed out the urns of brewed coffee and a display of Stollen, Aschener, Printen and Bethmannchen pastries. Although they had just eaten sandwiches and drank beer on the way over, they went after the coffee and sweets without hesitation. Warner sensed these men burned calories just sitting still. Despite their calm and polite exteriors, they seemed to exude a dangerous energy. He didn't know who made him more anxious, Michael Christian with his arrogant display of power and control over Warner's plant, or this new threesome. If he didn't know better, he would think they were gangsters.

Although Warner did not want to have conversation with them, it seemed more like they were ignoring him, than he was dismissive of them. They seemed very comfortable just waiting and were at ease in his space. That made him all the more ill at ease. Thank God the office door finally opened, and Christian walked out with Jentzil.

"I hope you find success Mr. Christian. I am sorry I could not be of more help to you." Jentzil walked out of the building without so much as a glance or a word to Warner.

Warner did not know what to think. When Jentzil exited Christian's office, Warner was certain that the group leader would have something revealing to offer to the investigation and that he would be naming employees involved. Now it seemed he had given nothing.

I, on the other hand, was thankful Jentzil dodged Warner, and he could not tell from my face just what did or didn't occur in that office over the last hour. I didn't want him to know that I had a short list of names to begin interviewing; a couple of drivers, an order entry clerk and a worker in the logistics department.

"Doctor Warner, make arrangements for your boiler operators, plant engineers and maintenance team to come to work at six a.m. tomorrow morning, but no sooner. They are to prepare the plant for opening. You are not to call your other workers and put them on standby until I tell you to do that. We are not out of the woods, not by a long shot. Regardless, I want the plant operational on a moment's notice. The prosecutor will not object and the police are aware not to interfere with your start-up operations. When you have notified your staff, you may go home. Come back late tomorrow morning, around ten a.m."

I sent Warner packing on his latest assignment and intentionally left him in the dark. As far as I was concerned, he was still a suspect. I glanced over at the three men having coffee and pastries as if they worked here.

I knew right away that these were my guys. I had seen that kind of poise before.

"Gentlemen, welcome. My name is Michael

Christian. Please refill your snacks and come in my office. We may be a while." I chuckled internally as one of the guys grabbed the entire pastry tray and one hoisted the coffee urn. The third grabbed all three mugs and stuck a fourth in his jacket pocket. I was guessing that was for me.

Before we could even sit down, my desk phone rang. It was Rutger Becker. He was about twenty minutes out. I called out to Warner to leave the front door to the admin building unlocked. Becker would see himself in, and when I told him I was camped out in Warner's office, he recalled having been there before.

I began my introduction. "I presume Morgan has told you who I am relative to the company. I am the global security executive. I have been sent here to fix a problem and you are my eyes, ears and hands for that. I am waiting for a Bundespolizei senior investigator to join us. He will be here in about fifteen minutes. So, let's use that time to give me some background on you guys. Why did Morgan pick you?"

They were pretty brief about their military backgrounds, but they gave me enough to be satisfied. Guys like these had no need to puff up their resumes. Kent took the lead with the introductions. He was a US citizen posted here by the State Department in Germany. Besides

English, he was fluent in five languages including Farsi, French, German, Polish and Russian. He would definitely be my voice relative to the German language and local customs. He had lived in Europe for over ten years, as both a civilian and as a solider. Although a federal employee, I guessed he was regularly "on loan" to Morgan.

Peter was a technical expert – computers, phones, eavesdropping, still and video cameras. He mentioned something about satellites but seemed to keep that intentionally vague. He too was a US State Department employee posted in Paris. He too had some "time to kill," so here he was.

Tyler then took over. He was a former military policeman who moved into the Special Forces group just prior to the start of the Gulf War. Although they all had combat and special mission experience, Tyler seemed to have some sort of informal rank the other two respected. He was the natural leader and there was no tension amongst them about it.

Tyler opened, "I will be supporting you and directing the team in any aspect of the investigation where you need depth. If we come up short, I will add staff as necessary. I have a Master's Degree in Business Management with a major in accounting. I will be able to assist you with your review of business records. Peter will go to the telephone closet and begin looking at the servers for unreported communications, especially in areas where you suspect improper activity. He has computer software to speed up the search and sort the data for us.

Kent will begin reviewing any key documents you provide where German is the language of the correspondence. He will riff them for relevance, translating only those that appear to help us in the investigation. I think he should also interview the guards or any key witnesses. Besides being multi-lingual, he is experienced in the art of interviewing and interrogation. I also brought a bag of tools just in case we need extra technical support. That's it from the fifty-thousand-foot level. Can you tell us exactly what is going on here?"

Sure enough, Tyler was also a U.S. State Department employee out of London and moonlighting for Morgan as needed. This was exactly what I expected. They had been generally briefed about my problem but had no details. It didn't stop them however from formulating a plan and tasking each other with roles and responsibilities. Now it was time to put a point on the tip of the spear. I decided not to inquire about their duties at State or their "tools."

"I will give you a fast overview. In a few

minutes Detective Becker of the Federal Police will join us and when he arrives we will go into more detail. He is the lead investigator and is on loan to us from the Prosecutor. The two of them have shut down our plant because of resistance they got from Warner, whom you have met, and from the works-union boss named Jürgen Jentzil, whom you just saw walk out of my office. I have met Becker and he seems like a good and competent guy, but I will ask for your opinion of that, once you have met him. I am sure he will be helpful, but make no mistake about it, he will report everything we say and do, and relay our plans and strategies back to the lead investigative prosecutor. Best if we keep some things to ourselves."

Kent said, "Becker, Becker. That name rings a bell, but I wonder if it is the same Becker I once knew. If so, we will be okay."

"In essence," I continued, "the German authorities believe employees here are involved in an international smuggling operation. We think cigarettes and liquor." I could see the amused smiles on this group's faces. As if to say, *you have us involved in something this benign*? I continued, "They also believe company drivers and trucks are facilitating the border crossings and are being supported by company shipping manifests and customs paperwork."

"When the Germans tapped out their investigative leads and still had no case, they came to Doctor Warner, the operations executive here, and sought his cooperation. Between Warner and the union boss, they closed ranks and denied the Feds access to employees, paperwork or any of our business processes.

"Becker and Felder, the prosecutor, took it on their own authority to close the plant in retaliation. Within a matter of days our customers were invoking their contractual penalty clauses for our failure to meet their just-in-time delivery requirements. We provide electronics for just about everything that rolls here in Europe. Now our customers' plants are cutting back on production and laying off shift workers as they await our parts. We are facing two million US dollars a day in penalties and I need to get this plant up and running as fast as we can." Kent whistled softly in a way that said *holy cow.* "In another week that cost will rise to three million a day. Solving their case is the promise I made to get my plant back."

Tyler noted, "I thought you told Warner to start the plant back up tomorrow?"

"Yes, it has been completely shut down for over a week. It will take twelve to twenty-four hours to bring the equipment, boilers and other heavy machines back online. Warner doesn't know it yet, but the prosecutor has granted me permission to begin the start up process in front of giving us the plant back totally. In exchange, I must bring him actionable results by tomorrow night. He wants case closure from me. I am hoping to provide some good witnesses and generally outline the steps in the smuggling organization. I can negotiate getting my plant back with that. And that, gentlemen, is where I will need your support.

"One more thing." I added. "The Feds think perhaps this has gone beyond tax-free cigarettes and booze. They mentioned something about guns."

"Guns?" Peter said. "Now we're talking." His smile was aped by the others. This had taken on a whole new level of interest for them.

"I am not sure how that fits in yet. He didn't go into details. I hope Becker will fill in some of those gaps. But it does explain the intensity with which the locals are pursuing this and the extreme measures they have taken to penalize the plant for not cooperating. Basically, they have put fourteen hundred people out of work, just to make a point. And I have to make good on my word, or the plant will be permanently closed as sure as I am standing here with you.

Guys, we have to find out who is involved and how they are doing it. And we must put an end to it. My sense of urgency is also because we are racking up a two million dollar a day cost to close this case."

Chapter Nine

TOBIAZ WAS RECALLING HOW HE thought his problems with the Russians could get no worse until he got that call a week ago. His mobile phone had chirped as he drove alone on a two-lane country road outside of Szczecin. It startled him out of his funk. He had been subconsciously driving on icy roads, but his mind was on his dilemma and not on the highway. The ringing jarred him. He hoped it was Karol.

"Tobiaz?" It was Ulrich. "Tobiaz, Tadeusz asked me to call. There has been trouble at the plant."

"What do you mean, trouble?" Tobiaz could not believe his problems could get worse.

"A federal investigation is going on. They are onto the operation. The police came to the plant and talked with JJ and Warner. The plant has been shut down this afternoon, but our next load is still on the docks. They sent everyone home and the police are not letting anyone enter the plant. Tobiaz, that load has our names on the delivery schedule. If they find out what is inside the crates ..."

It was more than Tobiaz could grasp. "What do you mean an investigation? Who is onto us? The plant is shut down? The *whole* plant? Ulrich, talk to me. This cannot be!"

"We do not have any details." Ulrich added. "We were driving back to the plant with the truck. When we got to the gate, the police were there with Karl, the guard. I asked him what was going on, but he just signaled with his eyes not to pursue it because the police officers were there. A policeman escorted us into the plant where we parked the truck at our usual dock. I could see inside the dock doors and our paperwork was already taped our crates."

"This was our biggest haul yet Tobiaz, and it is stuck on the dock. I tried, but they would not let us load it onto the truck. I tried explaining how important the delivery was for our customers. All they said was "*too bad*." They walked us over to the parking lot where we got into our cars and left."

"The guard said the plant will not open

tomorrow and we will not be driving. It seemed like he wanted to give us some information but could say nothing because the police were there. That is when Tadeusz told me to call you. He will talk with JJ to see what is going on. That is all we know. I will call you, or Tadeusz will, as soon as we learn more. Tobiaz, we may be finished here."

Tobiaz had been contemplating quitting anyway. This would have been the perfect out, except an investigation was going on and it was targeting their operation. This was possibly even worse than having Russian partners. Damn those Russians. Tobiaz would have to figure out what and how to tell them. He would have to call Anatoly. But first he would call Karol.

Karol did not pick up his call. So Tobiaz called the Russian. Anatoly's phone rang and rang. As much as Tobiaz hated talking with Anatoly, he had to have this conversation with him. "Pick it up you god damned Russian. Pick it up!"

▪ ▪ ▪ ▪ ▪

Anatoly's world was simple. He was a washed-out soldier. After the fall of the Soviet Union, the Russian army was no longer a place to earn a living, honest or otherwise. The opportunities were richer out on the street though. With his skills and training, he figured he could do better with the young toughs who were the newly emerging leadership of the *Russkaya Mafiya*, or Russian Mafia. He left active duty as soon as his draft was over.

After his military service, things didn't start out as smoothly for Anatoly as he thought they would. A good friend, who dabbled in counterfeit US dollars and served some time in prison, had grown rapidly in the mafia upon his release. Anatoly reached out to him expecting a high-level position. He was disappointed to learn that without having served a stint in prison himself and being *vetted* by fellow convicts, Anatoly would have to rise through the ranks on his own. It didn't matter who he knew, there was no way around that rule of entry. He was starting out lower than he had hoped. Thank God for Pavel.

Right now, he was drinking at a local pub frequented by newly rich Russians. Some of his *Bratva* buddies, made members, were there also. Anatoly still smelled of cigarettes and sweat. His friends were keeping him on the fringes, perhaps to keep their thousand-dollar suits from being soiled or stained. They flashed their wads of hundred-dollar bills in US currency and dropped one on the table for Anatoly as they walked off. He hated feeling like he was begging for scraps at the tables of the rich and famous. He would have to try another friend or more drastic measures if things didn't improve soon. His depression was interrupted by the incessant ringing of his phone.

Disgustedly, Anatoly answered, “Yes?”

Tobiaz could hear the sound of others talking in the background, “Anatoly, this is Tobiaz.”

“Why do you call me? I do not like to talk with you Tobiaz. When I want something from you, I call you.”

“Anatoly, there is an investigation. The German Federal Police …”

That is when Anatoly’s sphincter got tight and his senses awakened, “An investigation? Who? Into what? Into you? Into our business? What are you talking about Tobiaz. Talk to me!” Anatoly was trying to keep his voice down, but the anger and confusion came through clearly.

Maybe Tobiaz should have waited until Tadeusz had a chance to talk with his union boss. This would have given Tobiaz more information for Anatoly. But he knew better than to wait to call him. “Anatoly, I called you as soon as I heard about it. The plant is closed. The police are at the gates. The employees are not being allowed back into the plant. Ulrich said he saw tomorrow’s load already crated and on our dock, but we cannot get to it.”

"Your cousins have fucked this up Tobiaz. This is exactly why I want my people driving." Anatoly growled.

"This has nothing to do with my cousins Anatoly. Our routes had been flawless until you and your people came on the scene. We have successfully been moving our small loads without discovery or interruption and we have kept it within the family and a small circle of very close friends. Now you and Gennady come along, and we are discovered. I suggest you look inside your own circle to find out how this could have happened." Tobiaz was enraged and no longer cared about angering Anatoly. It didn't hurt that he was on the phone about one hundred eighty kilometers away either.

"Tobiaz, I expect that delivery on time. You must figure a plan to get it to me. No exceptions. The consequences will be bad for me if I do not deliver. They will be worse for you and your "*cousins*." He spewed out the word in bitter contempt.

Tobiaz could hardly contain himself. Torn between fear and anger, he spat into the phone, "I will call you when I have more, Anatoly," and abruptly hung up. This was typical of those Russian *wieprzowy*. God, he hated those pigs.

The Russian slammed down his phone on his table. He would have to call Gennady. It was time for drastic measures and these Poles needed to be dealt with.

Simultaneously, Tobiaz dialed Karol's phone again. Still no answer, so he left a voice message. "Karol, this is Tobiaz. Where are you? Please call me as soon as you get this message. I am worried sick, and there have been developments."

Tobiaz was desperate for Karol to pick up his calls. He needed assurances that Karol was all right. Not just for Karol's wife, but for his own satisfaction. Moreover, he was having trouble figuring this out on his own. Together he and his brother might be able to decide how to extricate themselves from the clutches of these vultures. Alone, they were no match for the Russians and they all knew it. Extreme measures were called for, but this was not who they were. His only option in the meanwhile was for Tadeusz and Ulrich to work something out at the plant and get that load off the docks. He needed to talk with Karol. If only he had another day.

Their load had been stuck on the dock for over a week now and he still had not heard from Karol. He feared the worst.

■ ■ ■ ■ ■

"Hello! Is anyone here?" Becker called out as he entered the lobby.

I rose and walked out to meet him. He was carrying a large legal briefcase. It looked heavy by the way he was carrying it.

"I come bearing gifts, Mr. Christian."

"Please call me Mike. Gifts?"

"Prosecutor Felder and I have decided that, since you are well vouched for, there is no sense in tying one hand behind your back. We both want the same end result, sort of." He pointed to his satchel, "Here, I have a copy of my complete investigative file. We will be sharing that with you."

I did not know what to say. Frankly, I was stunned. I was expecting quiet resistance, or at least passive aggressive cooperation, not such an open hand. I was warming to Becker already.

"Come join us. My team is in Warner's office which I have commandeered as an operations center."

"And Warner?" asked Becker looking around. It was obvious he did not care for or trust Warner.

"I sent him home. Right now, he is not on my list of good little boys."

When we entered my office, the trio was back at the pastry tray and refilling coffee. "Boys, I'd like you to meet Detective Rutger Becker."

At the mention of Becker's name, Kent's

head snapped up. Without turning he said "Rutger Becker? Berlin's own super star Stadtpolizei?" He turned and looked at Becker. When their eyes met, Becker dropped his briefcase and gave Kent a huge bear hug, lifting him off his feet.

"Kent, Kent, Kent. Mein Gott. You are alive!"

"Alive and well, my friend. And it looks like you have survived Stasi death squads and an assassination attempt also." Becker put him down as the group looked on, enjoying the camaraderie and awaiting an explanation.

Kent began, "I was assigned to the British Foreign Office and posted in Berlin before the wall came down. The spy game was active and aggressive. Both sides were using the scum of the earth as runners. It came to my attention that a new and rising star in the Stadtpolizei was on an East German gang hit list. He was kicking ass and breaking up cells faster than any of his predecessors, so the erstwhile rivals agreed to come together to take out our friend, Mr. Becker, here. I took a walk across the street to their offices and let them know what I had heard, who was at the heart of the threats, and offered any assistance we could muster. Remember, we were playing our intelligence sharing relationships very close to the vest, but the inside track was betting that Gorbachev was ready to tear down the wall and dissolve the Soviet Union at any time. Although we could share intelligence, we were not supposed to engage the East Germans nor do anything that might disrupt that forward progress.

"Herr Becker and I took a walk one day and hopped the wall. When we came back to the west side, the death threat problem was solved, at least on our side of the wall. There might have been a bit of a clean up required on the other side. Shortly after, I ended up in the Middle East and we lost touch. At least that's my story and I am sticking to it."

Becker stood there grinning and shrugging his shoulders, as if to suggest he had no idea what Kent was talking about. His subtle and humorous denial was confirmation enough.

Kent introduced Becker to the other members of his team with a promise to head to a beer hall as soon as possible. They could get caught up and introduce the guys more thoroughly then. Now, however, it was time to get down to work.

"Rutger, I have given the guys an overview of the problem covering both your and my goals of solving the case and getting the plant operating again. I did not go into any depth about the arms thing. Frankly, I really don't know anything at all about it. Nor do I have any details about how you became aware of the smuggling, or even the extent it is occurring. How about you take over from here?"

Rutger opened the big black leather satchel and extracted a thick stack of notes, two-hole punched and bound at the top with expandable wire brackets. The long strands didn't seem to have much expansion left in them. "Rather than go into a page by page account of my notes, let me summarize the key sections."

"We received a tip from a small-time burglar we busted for a jewelry store break-in. This last arrest had him looking at hard time, for multiple offenses. He wanted to cut a deal and offered a bigger fish, as he called it."

"He said he fenced all his easily identifiable jewels in Rostock to try to stay under our radar in Berlin and Hamburg. It was in Rostock he learned of a smuggling ring working out of Reinbeck. These guys supposedly dropped partial loads at the docks in Rostock and then drove the rest into Poland. That is where your employees come in, Mike. He said the crews delivered from your plant and that someone inside was forging customs paperwork and bills of lading for local deliveries. He tried to connect with these guys but couldn't.

He had no names, but his knowledge about the drop locations, the plant here in Reinbeck and the means they used for getting through highway inspections and border crossings was enough to get us started. It seemed to make sense to us since we were already looking at smuggling from this plant – just not at guns.

"The first step we took was to covertly try and identify the logistics drivers and routes. That was an enormous undertaking, given the size of your operations. Do you know that you have twenty-six docks that are operational twenty-four/seven?"

"I know that those docks are silent right now." That was probably a bit too edgy given the generosity of his information sharing. "Sorry Rutger. No, I didn't know the total scope of our operations, but I expect we will shortly walk the grounds to see what we can learn."

Becker continued. "You appear to have an in-house driver pool of over twenty people serving short hauls, local runs, long hauls and cross border deliveries. In addition, you also have somewhere on the order of five different third-party carriers."

"How do you have all these details if you received no cooperation from plant officials?" I asked.

"Good question. We started with surveillance on the gates. We could not get a good view of the docks from our vantage points because they are inside the fence line and obscured by trees and other buildings. It took days of sitting and copying down the cab and trailer names and numbers, and their license plate numbers. Our inside teams ran all those names and numbers to give us the general information. Since all the trucks are corporate registrations, we did not have any driver information. We counted inbound and outbound vehicles and their times. Fortunately, your plant has separate gates for receiving raw materials and supplies and another for shipping, so we were able to isolate deliveries."

"A major challenge we faced was trying to understand what third-party delivery trucks entered the plant completely empty and which were carrying partial loads from other customers on their routes. We had to make some general assumptions. We did not have the manpower to follow all these vehicles, especially when we did not know which vehicles were heading where and with what loads. That is when we approached your Warner and Jentzil."

"And that is when they told you to pound sand?" I interrupted.

"Pound sand?" He asked.

"Sorry Rutger. It is an American expression. It means go bugger off." Kent smiled at my use of the British version of the expression.

Becker grinned in understanding and agreement. “Yes, they told me to go bugger off.”

He continued, “I warned them that we were very serious about the investigation and that we had every reason to believe that insiders in the plant were complicit. But Warner was insistent that he would know if something untoward was going on. He said he had just been audited and all was in order.

“Jentzil told me it didn’t matter. He felt the government was on a witch-hunt and without us requesting specific people to interview, he was not going to advise the workers to cooperate. He went even further. He said he would advise the workers not to answer our questions without a court order.”

“That got under my skin, I am afraid. It wasn’t the first time I had been told to pound sand. But I was expecting more support from a major corporation. I thought to myself, *We shall see who pounds sand my friends*. I returned to my office and explained all to Herr Felder.”

I asked, “And the two of you just decided to close the plant? Did you not wonder about all these workers losing their jobs?”

“Oh, yes we did. We talked about the options. Our investigation was at a stalemate. We were not going to receive any further investigative funds. We had watched the place for days with dozens of officers round the clock. We borrowed members from the gang squad, the burglary details, and the highway commission. But without any more than a snitch's word, we had to return all our resources. We considered that the plant management, when faced with a court order to close the plant, would have a change of heart and begin producing paperwork and witnesses. But no! Warner dug in his heels and we began receiving intimidating phone calls from your European counsel."

"Yes," I mused out loud. "That would be their style. We are among the twenty-five largest corporations in the world. The attorneys are not used to being pushed around."

"Yes. So, given the lack of cooperation and the resistance from Warner and Jentzil, and the heavy handedness of your lawyers, Herr Felder and I dug our heels in as well. And that brings us to where we are today."

"Not quite Rutger. This still does not explain the gun smuggling allegations. What is that all about?" I asked.

"This is not as tight a connection," He replied. "But here is what we have.

"We ran our general information by our friends at Interpol to see if they had information to share on any smuggling operations from

Reinbeck to Poland. They said they did not have anything out of Reinbeck, but they had received several undocumented reports of a smuggling operation out of the Warnemunde dock area of north Rostock. Perhaps you are unaware of the area, but Warnemunde is a port town about thirty-five minutes north of Rostock. Although it is a tourist area, it is still a large and active cargo harbor."

"They had no details, no good informant, no leads and no way to connect our interest to their investigation. So rather than reach out to us as the case was developing, they merely cross-referenced their information into a general Interpol information file about Rostock and Warnemunde. When I mentioned that the trucks in our investigation might have left from Reinbeck to Rostock, they became most interested. They said their suspicions were that guns were making their way through Rostock or Warnemunde and into Russia."

"Although it was exciting to hear that, we still had no direct connection between their vague intelligence and our investigation. I surmised that their case was based on source information. Possibly the same source we had developed. So, we crossed referenced our files and that was the end of it. To this point, we still have not been able to make a connection."

He continued, “Given neither they, nor we, had any specific details, we agreed to keep each other posted if anything concrete came of our investigation. That is why we felt it necessary to put pressure on your management, seeking their support in the investigation. Yes, with access to witnesses, documents and your processes, perhaps we would already be at the conclusion. If all we got was cigarettes and liquor, fine. But we all had that gut feeling we might be on to something more.” Becker concluded and waited for a reaction.

I understood gut feelings. From the intense interest showing on the faces of my team, I got the feeling they did too. “So Rutger, if you could interview our employees. Whom would you start with?” I was playing with him a bit to see where the investigation would go if we gave him access, or if he was just bluffing at this stage of the game. I wanted to be sure he wasn’t just trying to catch a break.

“I would start with the drivers and see what kind of reaction we get. Maybe one of them would break or give a tell-tale indicator of guilty knowledge. I would also talk with your shipping people. Regardless, unless we got something concrete, Felder and I could not even mount a surveillance. We just do not have the resources anymore."

My concern mounted at that point. If they could not get investigative support, the plant could be closed indefinitely. But his scope of interviews was too great. With twenty drivers, it would not only *appear* to be a witch hunt, it *would* be one in every respect.

He tossed the ball back into my court. "What do you propose to do Mike? It is now your commitment that moved Herr Felder to re-open the plant. I am sure he would like to know at least the outline of your plan."

I was ready for that. I had been considering what to share with Rutger. But with Kent vouching for him and with what seemed to be an open and frank exchange of information I decided to go ahead with what I had in mind.

"Okay Rutger," I responded. "You have given us some insight and Tyler and the crew have an overall plan of attack as well. Here is what I am thinking."

"If we map out what we know or surmise, a process emerges. At some point shipping and customs paperwork must be generated for each crate that is put on a truck for delivery. That process is automated and links to our production runs. This process is not only what authorizes a truck out of our gates, but it tells the forklift operators in the plant what to put onto which truck, and at which dock."

"Each driver is accountable for not only what is on each truck, but for making sure it is signed for when delivered. It is how we keep them honest."

"Warner has already gathered some of the paperwork I have asked for. These guys and I will go through it, but with an eye toward the vulnerability points. That should lead to some names. Already we know that we have to interview the order entry, logistics, and shipping folks. But I want to wait until we understand the paperwork and data entry processes a little better. We should also take that walk about and see what the place really looks like from the ground."

"I also believe we should be talking with the logistics manager soon, possibly even this evening. Rutger, we may need some fast work on background checking some of these folks. Do you have any resources?" I asked.

His answer was encouraging, "Yes, I can get very prompt feedback for just about anything in Germany. It may take a little longer if we are dealing with immigrant workers. I believe this plant has plenty of them."

Kent spoke up. "I may be able to shake a few trees for priority handling at Interpol. I know a few folks there too." He looked at Peter who nodded in assent. Very subtle and very understated but hinting more and more that these guys on my team were more than just pretty faces.

"Alright then. Let's get started." I went to the outer office where Warner had placed several stacks of folders for us. I could see the multi-colored tabs denoted employee files, customer orders, shipping and operational files.

Tyler joined me, and we carried the piles into my office and spread them on the conference room table.

Becker rose, "I have to get back to my office to close out a few things this evening. I will call in the morning before I come over. You have my home number and my mobile number, Mike. Call me if you need anything, any time of the night. By the way, I like the way you are keeping Warner at a distance. Even if uninvolved, he is still a pompous ass."

I smiled as I rose to shake his hand. "See you in the morning Rutger. And bring something with lots of sugar please. We will likely be running hard all night."

There was no raising of their eyebrows, no looks of disappointment or discontent from my three new team members. They each grabbed a pile of folders and began organizing them by type. I joined them with a fresh cup of coffee and did likewise.

We organized the files into manageable and logical piles. One for orders, one for inventory release and job numbers, one for manufacturing and assembly work orders, one for final packaging and staging, one for logistics drayage and one for billing. There was a final pile that included the personnel files of the key workers in each of those functions, managers and supervisors or senior shift leaders. The guards were from a third-party service, but the security supervisor had pulled together a list, naming each officer by shift and function. That would help too.

I erased everything off Warner's white board and mapped out the process flow for this facility, drawing boxes for various points along the way. It was very similar to our operations in Detroit and Pittsburgh. I knew from many past experiences that the operational process was the link to where the internal controls breakdown. And employees with access at those vulnerability points were either involved or had guilty knowledge. The challenge was to find those gaps in controls and then find out who had been exploiting them. The written process looked something like this...

Raw materials and rough parts entered the plant through security at the receiving gate. The guards validated the bills of lading against a logistics sheet to ensure the order was expected and being delivered by the intended freight company. The security officer then called the receiving office to get a dock assignment for the truck to unload.

The forklift operator confirmed the offloaded contents against the freight bill and the parts were then entered into inventory. This also confirmed the legitimacy of a future invoice by the freight company and by the supplier.

When a customer ordered parts, the order entry department confirmed the customer was properly enrolled in the billing system and set up for payment against a contract or a sales record. Order entry then generated a job number authorizing parts from inventory, manufacturing, and assembly. The work orders were linked to the job numbers for parts that ended up on a shipping document and on a later invoice.

When finished parts were ready to be shipped, the logistics department was notified to arrange delivery. Logistics determined whether to use company drivers or third-party drivers. If company drivers were used, logistics determined which crews and routes they would have. Forklift operators staged and loaded the crated parts onto trucks at their assigned docks and in the order of delivery, if there were multiple stops. The forklift operator and the truck driver confirmed the crate count before the doors were locked and sealed. The driver signed off on the forklift operator's work order and the forklift operator signed off on the driver's manifest.

The guards inspected the driver's paperwork to ensure all is in order before the truck could leave the plant.

Once that process flow chart hit the white board, we began placing the files in the right order on the table. We then placed personnel jackets next to the key points in the process piles. Some things became obvious right away, but I want to see the place personally before I jumped to any conclusions.

"Listen guys, before we tackle the paperwork, I think it is time to stretch our legs and take a walk, or a ride as the case may be. This is a big piece of property."

Tyler spoke up. "I've got a seven-passenger vehicle out there with plenty of cargo space. We can go in that."

"Okay." I said. "You drive. Stop at the front guard house first. I want to let him know we will be out and about."

It would also give us a chance to come to some conclusion about his trustworthiness. Very often a guard was part of the process of illegally getting trucks and assets out of the plant. Or his incompetence was a major contributor.

Chapter Ten

PAVEL OVESHKIN WAS A HAPPY MAN. HE preferred his Cuban cigars sweet, his whiskey aged and his women young, very young. His wealth allowed him to enjoy all his predilections.

Oveshkin was once a highly regarded soldier and was appointed by Russian Commander Bogdan Matveev to administer the East Berlin armory. The armory was located just outside of East Berlin and his quarters were very close to Humbolt University. He loved this assignment, not only because of his officer's status, pay, responsibility and the visibility it afforded him, but because the University was home to so many pretty young students. He was handsome, muscular in a military officer's way, and he had an official car. His rank and location both served him well with the young students.

And he did have one special, pretty young girl he was seeing there, but that would all end with his re-assignment to Russia.

A massive accumulation of Soviet weapons, soldiers and their families was built in the towns around Berlin. The contingent of personnel alone was estimated to be nearly one million people. Plans were immediately begun to invade West Germany and then all of Europe. But the undertaking ran out of time. Gorbachev tore down the wall.

Once the plan to invade West Berlin had failed and the Soviet Union had been dismantled, Oveshkin was forced to make his plan to leave the German Democratic Republic and to leave the military service. The movement of all those soldiers back to Russia meant there would be no homes or jobs for them. Oveshkin knew he would soon regress from being respected, to being scorned and ostracized. Regardless of his rank, he had no home to return to in Russia and his economic future was in doubt. The demise of the Soviet Union and thus his role in East Berlin took place over three, very fast years.

The Russians began a controlled exodus of their troops and their families. They also took with them everything that wasn't nailed down and took much of that too. Besides that, the pressure on him was immense to ensure the security of the weapons and ammunition while they figured out how and where to transport it.

If anything, though, Pavel was creative under pressure. He quickly realized that he was one of only a few people fully aware of the current contents of the armory. His first order was to conduct and report an inventory to Matveev. Then he was ordered to devise a logistics strategy for delivering the weapons to the armory in St. Petersburg. Once there, the goods were out of Pavel's hands. He began a process that required the removal of over seven hundred-thousand tons of weapons, munitions and explosives among other things. His goal was to leave not a single bullet behind.

The queries from headquarters were often filled with panicked vagaries. Pavel could tell they had no idea of the specific quantities of weapons and soon a plan of another type began to emerge.

The closest seaport was Warnemunde. The journey from there to St. Petersburg was twelve hundred and eighty-seven kilometers up the Baltic Sea, and the land route to Moscow was eighteen hundred kilometers. There was no way to ensure that such a delivery over a land route was completely secure by truck or by rail. Or so he told those at headquarters. Running full out, a loaded cargo ship averaged about twenty-five knots per hour. It would take about two days to get from Rostock to St. Petersburg and the cargo would be intact all the way.

Although they agreed to use both transit paths, the sea-lane served Pavel's private purposes best. He could also make use of the short rail service from Berlin to Warnemunde or run the rails through Poland to Moscow. Everyone liked the plans so much they put Pavel in charge of the shipments, end-to-end. He was now in charge of the inventory count, security of the armory, packaging, containerizing, ground and sea transportation and logistics. Separation of duties was not a business principle that seemed to matter. That fit into Pavel's ambitions just fine.

Pavel had been seeing a young girl from Humbolt University. Tasha was a University freshman and had barely celebrated her eighteenth birthday when he started seeing her. She was impressed that he had a car and a private housing unit on the base where they could meet. She learned about sexual pleasures of all kinds from Pavel, and she hungered for the experiences she had been told were only enjoyed by dirty girls. Pavel taught her them all. But he preferred it when they could get away altogether, away from the eyes of the educators, from his supervisors and from Tasha's young girlfriends.

Often Pavel would drive her, in his convertible military car, to Plau am See, about two hours north. Plau am See was more like a small village than a town. It offered privacy and anonymity, and he had to admit it was almost cozy. Tasha's aunt had a home with a small dock and a rowboat there and Tasha liked to take evening boat rides along the shore. Although it did not mean much to Pavel, Tasha was a romantic and enjoyed the quiet time. It also seemed to make her more energetic and pliable after time on the water and that suited him just fine.

They stayed at Tasha's aunt's lakeside residence whenever the old lady was gone for the weekend and soon he came to be comfortable there. He enjoyed the privacy it offered. Unlike his barracks unit, he could loudly screw a college freshman all day without interruption or fear of being overheard.

They would stay in bed the entire weekend if it were up to him, except she had a desire to walk along the back roads through the small lakeside town. It was there Pavel discovered the north-south railroad tracks that ran along the west side of the town center. And that is where he found the abandoned warehouse with its own rail siding. It would serve him well. Warnemunde was accessible on those tracks and it was so close. More importantly, Warnemunde was a place of opportunists, and what Pavel needed right then were some other opportunists.

It wasn't long before Pavel was shipping the armory inventory on a regular basis, literally as fast as they could be crated, to St. Petersburg and to Moscow. But he also controlled the drayage opportunities and the associated paperwork. Pavel used Tasha's cousin Misha, in Plau am See, to accept sided crates and move them into the lakeside warehouse. Although Misha did not know what was in the crates, he knew they contained stolen property. These munitions never made it to Russia, at least not to their rightful owners. These were Pavel's guns now and they were kept in the abandoned warehouse for safekeeping. It was only a short matter of time before he found buyers for the weapons within the Russian Mafia and emerging Muslim rebel groups in Chechnya and beyond.

Within months Pavel began rising from a moderately well-off military perfunctory to a very wealthy man. The movement of his weapons had gone on for the final eight months until the armory was empty. It was then that his luck changed. He was abruptly pulled from Berlin and was being returned to St. Petersburg. Basically, he was transferred to an administrative desk job once his service from the armory was completed. He wasn't being downgraded in rank. But he was losing opportunity. Most importantly, he was losing access to his assets.

His knew his day-to-day trysts with Tasha would be coming to an end and he saw her occasionally. He was relying long-distance on Misha to facilitate driving his guns to Warnemunde. He needed to keep that connection alive. Once in Warnemunde, he had friends who would unload and guard his goods until he could get them to his customers, by boat or by truck.

Unfortunately for Pavel, Misha developed a drug problem, financed mostly through the *found money* he was being paid for helping Oveshkin. The young man had to flee the local polizei and he hid out in the big city of Berlin, fearing imprisonment if he returned to Plau am See. Oveshkin saw Misha as a loose end. He couldn't trust a junkie to keep his hands off of Pavel's weapons.

And that is how Pavel's crates of munitions came to sit inaccessible to him while he was in Russia. His connection had literally fled the scene. He was eighteen hundred kilometers away from his source of hot cash and that was a serious dilemma. That is, until sweet little Tasha mentioned, in a love letter, her new job as an order entry clerk at an international automotive manufacturing company in Reinbeck. He wondered how else he could use her talents to meet his goals. Pavel's creativity was remarkable, he thought. And little Tasha thought he was such a charmer.

He called her to discuss the chance to move his guns out of Plau am See with legitimate paperwork. When she told how easy it would be, he was thrilled. He contacted his trusted friends Anatoly, Gennady and Yevgeny and put them to work. It was messy to involve so many people, but for now it was necessary. As in everything he managed, he immediately began planning to clean up all his loose ends. Misha was Pavel's first assignment for Anatoly and Gennady. Soon his would be a very efficient operation again.

He would have sent for Tasha. She used to know how to make him feel so alive. But she was almost twenty now and she was getting too old for him. New days called for new little birds and now he could afford an entire flock.

Chapter Eleven

THERE WAS HARDLY ANY WIND ALONG the back property line of the plant. It made the early evening cold tolerable, as did the heat we generated from walking. The four of us had checked in with Karl, the front gate guard before we embarked on our plant-tour. The officer gave us a two-way radio in case we needed anything from him. He seemed friendly enough and quite forthcoming about the process he used to check trucks out of the facility. He took his business seriously and showed us copies of truck activity logged onto the sheets we had briefly scanned earlier. We discovered something by visualizing him work, rather than by reviewing his log sheets.

When the officer exited the booth to examine a trucker's papers, there was no seal inspection because the doors were not locked as the drivers approached the gate. They were left open for the officer to examine the contents against the manifest. The officer did not examine contents in any detailed manner, he merely looked inside the truck from ground level, then looked at the paperwork to see the forklift operator's signature. After that, he passed the vehicle through. When we asked him about the seals, he said that was up to the driver to affix. He merely looked to see the numbers matched. That was vulnerability number one.

There was nothing particularly unusual about the grounds as we passed the receiving docks and the front of the main manufacturing plant. These were solidly constructed brick over concrete buildings, with minimum windows, except in the front offices. All the landscaping was clean. The tree branches had been cut high from the ground and the shrubbery had been cut low creating a sight-line. Everything would be neat again in the spring and ground cover in bare spots would grow no more than four inches. The fence line was in good repair throughout. Gates had clean, functional chains, but they were not all locked. It was while walking the fence line that we noticed the next oddity and vulnerability number two.

Sparkling clean electronic ignitions, wire harnesses and distributor assemblies were strewn between the fence line and the tree line. The clear zone was littered with parts. This was obviously going on for a while, as some of the parts had varying degrees of rust, but so many were clean. *Why? What were these parts doing here and how did they get here? And, why did the guard not notice on his patrol rounds?* Christian wondered. It was a question that begged an answer.

"Tyler, when we get back, I want you to interview the guard and get an answer to these parts being out here. I don't want to go into a management interview without first talking with the guard and getting his statement on record."

Tyler nodded his understanding. Kent took some photos. I had seen new, clean parts lying in the grass of other plants. I knew this was the carelessness of employees stealing parts for their scrap value or their resale value. I was guessing this was going on at the Reinbeck plant as well. My instincts and experiences were likely spot on in this case. These parts probably had nothing to do with the smuggling case. Nevertheless, if employees could steal random parts, there was a weakness in parts inventory management. This led me to believe the smuggling facts were likely real as well. We moved on.

The fence line had a gate that led to a yard that was also enclosed by a fence. It looked like a storage yard with a half dozen wooden shipping crates. As we pushed on the crates, we could tell they were full. Plastic sheets containing computer generated shipping labels were stapled to the outside of each crate. The dates were as recent as a week ago, and their destinations were generally to the north or east side of the country. They fit the profile of shipments containing contraband. We wondered aloud if these were the illegal shipments. Kent recorded the shipper info into his notebook and took more pictures.

"Okay, Tyler," I said, "add this to your list of questions for the guards. Why are these here?"

Peter was looking around on the ground and returned momentarily with a metal plate. It looked like a mini pry bar. Within a minute, he had the lid off a crate. Inside was nothing but boxes of automotive parts wrapped in oiled shipping paper or in OEM boxes. We opened a dozen of them at least.

"Unless there are liquor bottles under all these boxed parts, I am guessing these are legitimate parts scheduled for delivery." Peter said. "We won't know until we empty a crate or two. How about if Kent and I get about it. You guys keep going and we will catch up."

Tyler and I nodded our assent and moved on.

The grounds were eerily empty considering the place employed over fourteen hundred workers across three shifts. Other than the guards at the gates, we had yet to come across anyone else. Given the place was closed, we didn't expect much more.

The air had picked up out of the north and had a deeper bite as dusk settled in. I could feel it now as it nipped under my collar. We approached the shipping docks at the far end of the property and Tyler hopped briskly up the stairs and tried the dock door. He gave the knob a turn and pulled on it. The door opened. No alarms. We looked at each other in surprise. I guess we both expected the place to be buttoned down, especially the shipping docks. This is where finished goods got staged for delivery.

Inside, each dock doorway had been painted on the floor with lanes that served as drop zones for shipping cartons. There were only two that had crates staged, awaiting shipment. My guess was that the deliveries never got off the dock once the Federal Police shuttered the place. Tyler copied down the crate shipping label information and we moved on.

Normally abuzz with the whining of forklift engines, cranes, and pneumatic hammers the two hundred thousand square feet of warehouse-shipping space was now dead silent.

We did an eye scan of the place to confirm it was empty and left, not locking the door behind us.

As we approached the gatehouse for the shipping drivers I noticed something amiss. The rear guard was not in attendance. Instead his post was being staffed by a uniformed Stadtpolizei police officer. It was the same motorcycle cop, in the high polished boots, who Friedrich had been talking with outside my office window. Rutger didn't say anything about switching out security for cops. This was too much of a coincidence to be a coincidence. Besides, I don't believe in them anyway.

As we approached the gatehouse from inside the grounds, the officer spotted us. “Guten Tag. Wie kann ich dir helfen?” he asked in German.

I didn’t know much German but knew a few key phrases. “Sprichst du English?” I asked.

“Ein Bischen,” he replied. “A little.” His mood changed from conversational to confrontational.

Something was amiss. He didn’t know I recognized him from earlier and he seemed not to recognize me. I thought I better get the jump on him with attitude, so I demanded of him. "Who are you and what you are doing here? Where is our security guard?"

He took his time responding and seemed to be trying to size us up. The darkness outside the gates didn't help him much in that regard. "Who are *you*?" He pushed back, avoiding my question.

"I'm from corporate headquarters in the United States. We own this facility. I repeat my question. Where is our security guard?"

He seemed taken aback because I didn't back down and in Tyler he saw the eyes of a professional sizing him up.

"We are taking over security at this facility until the issue is resolved." He stated.

"Who is taking over the facility? And what issue are you talking about?"

He seemed confused about how to answer. He balked, not knowing how much I knew or didn't know and he could tell that I wasn't offering any information about my presence or my role. He also didn't seem to have an explanation beyond the fact that he was a law enforcement figure and was exerting his authority.

"The federal government has decided that it is best if we manage the security of this facility.

Tomorrow the rest of my crew will be here staffing all the gates."

"Does the front gate security officer know about this?" I asked. It seemed odd that the officer didn't mention this to us.

"He was to be notified. I made Officer Kirsch aware when I replaced him."

I wondered why a log-off protocol wasn't followed for Kirsch to leave the gate and to check in with the front gate officer that he was going home. I decided it made better sense for me to leave this guy in place and not scare him off. Something was up and his presence was part of it. I could tell Tyler sensed it as well. He was scoping out the BMW police motorcycle. I couldn't get close enough to the cop to see the engraved badge number on his uniform and the officer was not wearing a name plate on his jacket. I wasn't sure if that was protocol or because he was out of his authorized realm. We were going to find out, and fast.

"Well, we appreciate your concern. We will make sure the officer knows to expect your people in the morning." I nodded to Tyler who had completed his mission. We turned and walked back to the interior of the plant grounds.

When Tyler was sure we were out of earshot he said, "That's bullshit. Something's up. If Rutger was going to replace the security guards with polizei, I am sure he would have given us the heads up. Besides, he's turning the plant back over to us in the morning. Adding a police contingent seems a bit late at this stage. If you like, I'm sure I can get a straight story out of that cop in just a few minutes, if he is a cop."

"Oh, I think he is a cop. I saw him this morning outside my office window talking with my driver. I'm not sure yet about the driver, but he seems to be a straight up guy. It was the cop who was acting a bit out of character. Call Rutger and get this cleared up. And let's not tell the front gate guard just yet. If Kirsch did inform the gatehouse that he was leaving and that a cop was there, I want to know why we were not informed. But again, better to know the answer before we ask the question. Start with Rutger."

"OK, I'm on it."

"And one more thing." I added. "I'd like to get a set of eyes on this gate without the cop knowing we are watching. Is that something we can do, or do we need more people?"

"I did a little scoping out when I was walking around the cycle." Tyler said casually as if he did this all the time. "I think we can get a car positioned to see both up and down the road without being spotted and that can happen now, if you don't mind going a bit short handed in the paperwork department. In about an hour and a half, I can have a surveillance guy or two in place, in a non-descript van. That will get our core guys back in the office for the interviews."

"Okay." I said. "Let's get the surveillance started now and beefed up as soon as you can. Make sure they can roll and that they have the necessary paperwork to get them across a border if necessary. I think I have a plan."

We stopped by the front guard office and returned his radio. He still didn't say anything about the rear gate guard being off duty or the cop being there. He appeared innocently oblivious to the change. Or so it seemed.

When we got back to the office, I was surprised to see Peter interviewing a woman in the outer office. He looked up only briefly as Tyler and I entered and walked back to our office. We didn't interrupt.

Before I could ask what was going on, Kent closed the door behind us. "That's Tasha out there. She's the gal almost singularly responsible for creating customer order paperwork. She initiates production on the shop floor by generating customer order releases. That is the document that authorizes raw materials to be manufactured or for finished goods to be prepared for customer delivery. She coordinates with manufacturing, raw materials inventory, the finished goods warehouse and the shipping department."

"She is also responsible for returning goods to inventory if a customer refuses or cancels an order. Seems almost too good to be true that one person has that much unchecked responsibility. And she is so very young for that much unsupervised control. Once we figured that out, we were going to call her. But no sooner did we reach that conclusion, than in she walked. She said Warner called her and told her to get over here right away. She checked with the union guy, Jentzil, and he agreed, telling her to come right over. So, she did. I can tell you she is scared shitless."

It impressed me that Warner called her on his own. Did he think she was a co-conspirator and needed interrogating? Or did he think she might be the most helpful person to explain the order of business, given we were taking Warner out of the loop of trusted persons?

Kent continued, "She started out with denials of any knowledge, then gave inconsistent answers about processes she was in charge of. These should have been the easy questions for her. She was avoiding complete answers and was having trouble with eye contact. She had to repeatedly correct herself when Peter caught her in conflicting answers. He has caught her in so many lies that she has lost her poise and confidence and is forgetting her previous answers."

"She is either part of this or has guilty knowledge. Either way, she is in good hands. Peter will get something out of her and won't even have to lay a hand on her. He has already moved into her personal space. If you ask me, she is about ready to crack." His subtle reference to Peter not needing to use force didn't go unnoticed, but I ignored the comment.

"Thanks, Kent. You made some notes about the shipping papers stapled to the crates in the yard and Tyler has some information about crates we found on the loading docks in the shipping building. Let's see if we can reconcile some of this. Meanwhile, Tyler has a few calls to make."

"And by the way, there is a Stadtpolizei officer staffing the back gate. He said he was stationed there by Felder's office. We both think that's bullshit. Something's up. Tyler wants one of you guys in a car to watch that gate while he rounds up a surveillance crew. He is also calling Rutger to verify that cop's story about being placed there under federal orders to replace our guards."

"Okay, great." Kent said enthusiastically. "Looks like we are moving forward. I would expect that the shipping guy should be in soon too, if Warner got the order entry gal here that fast. I will get on those shippers. Comparing them for similarities should only take a few minutes. Then I will head out to the gate."

"You've got the keys, so get back to the rear gate." Tyler reminded Kent. "We need the analysis of the shippers from the dock crates and the yard crates right away, so I'll get on that. If something is going on with the crates, it is going on through that back gate and we don't want to miss it, so you get eyes on that. As soon as I finish here, I will give you a call on your mobile."

Kent grabbed his jacket and was out the door. Tyler was soon talking with one of his own contacts and I could tell it wasn't Morgan. Tyler seemed to have some horsepower of his own in Morgan's organization. These were no-hesitation, take-charge guys. I like that.

"Tyler, I'll call Rutger while you are handling the surveillance guys." I said.

I grabbed Rutger's business card with his mobile number and dialed.

He picked it up on the first ring. "Hello Rutger, this is Michael Christian. I hope I am not disturbing a fine dinner somewhere."

"No, you are not. How may I help you?"

"Well, there have been some developments and I wanted to bring you up to date. We also need some clarification about the local polizei and the role they are playing."

"The Stadtpolizei? What do you mean? They have no role. Why do you ask?"

"Well Rutger, we have had an interesting development. There is a police officer guarding the back gate. He said he was ordered there to support the federal investigation. He sent our guard home. He also said that in the morning, the rest of his team would arrive to relieve all our other security guards. Tyler and I both think something is up, but just wanted to confirm with you first. Did you order the polizei to take over security here?"

"Of course not. We gave you back your plant. Why would we want to guard it? I will have members of the federal task force over there in minutes to detain the officer for questioning. Something is up. We did not order this and the Stadtpolizei would coordinate any such activity through me personally. I can assure you that did not happen. Thank you for letting me know."

"Hold on a minute please, Rutger. You're right. Something is up, and we think the officer is a part of it. We believe we have also found something amiss here. There are crates of goods destined for locales similar to your smuggling routes. These crates have been hidden in a remote area of the grounds. We opened a crate to sample it and it appears to contain a legitimate parts order. We also found crates on the loading dock in the closed shipping department. The crates seem to have the same locales. We are researching that as we speak. If I am right, the crates on the dock contain contraband but have legitimate paperwork to ship them. I am guessing the order got stranded on the docks when you shut the place down. Now our suspects are making an effort to get inside the plant and get those crates through the rear gate, guarded by your officer. In a few minutes I will have fixed surveillance up and running on that gate. In about an hour, I will have a mobile surveillance in place in case those goods move. I would love to get the drivers and the buyers all in one night's activity. Can you lend me a surveillance crew?"

"Mike, that is amazing and so fast. Let's go through this again. No, I cannot get you a surveillance crew, at least not tonight. Perhaps tomorrow night. But before we go any further let me be perfectly clear about something. I do not hear you asking me about a member of the police department taking unauthorized action at your facility. If you had reported such a thing to me, I would be obligated to notify our equivalent of your Internal Affairs Bureau in the States to bring him in for questioning immediately. This might queer the investigation. Is that how you say it?"

I chuckled inwardly. "I guess you could say it that way. And no, I do not recall making any such observation to you either. And thank you Rutger. I understand and appreciate your position. I will keep you appraised as we move along. We are also interviewing someone we believe to be a key witness. She is in charge of most materiel movement other than the shipping department."

"Give me her name Mike. I'll check her out and get back with you." I covered the mouthpiece and told Tyler to get Tasha's identifying information. He went straight for the door. A moment later, he was back with a sheet from a note pad. On it was written Tasha's name, birthdate and a former married name. The note also had a note scribbled on it: *Kent is already checking her out with his resources.*

I passed the info on to Rutger, not wanting to share Kent's access to intelligence resources. I would be curious to see who got back to me first.

Rutger added, "Check in with me if it appears your people are going to have to cross a border. I can be of assistance getting them across."

I decided I would wait to see if Tyler's crew

needed or asked for assistance before calling Rutger. He was a good guy but bound by his own internal bureaucracies. And my guys seemed pretty good so far at getting things done.

I made one more request of Rutger, before we disconnected. “Tyler got the motorcycle cop’s license plate and unit number off his bike. Can you find out who this guy is?”

“Of course, Mike, have Tyler get me the number.”

Tyler overheard that part of the conversation and anticipated me. He handed me the information and I passed it along to Rutger. “Please call me as soon as you have anything Rutger. I will do likewise with you.”

We made our goodbyes and hung up.

Tyler was still making calls, so I went to the outer office. Peter was still talking with Tasha who looked like she had been crying. Kent motioned me over to his desk and away from Peter and Tasha.

“The shippers on both sets of crates are identical. I think your hunch is correct. The crates on the docks are for the smugglers. The presence of the cop suggests he is there to facilitate getting inside the plant. Tyler said you found the dock doors unlocked, so that will make it really easy.” I was glad to see that the guys were seeing it unfold the same way I did.

Kent continued, “I am just about to head out, but wanted to pass along something to you. We haven’t done a deep dive yet, but Tasha Krause is Natasha Boryenko. She is a resettled Russian who moved to East Germany as a child. She went to college in East Berlin and got a job as a translator for the Stasi in the German Democratic Republic. When the wall came down, she came to the western side under the name Tasha Krause and got a job here rather than return to Russia. Her papers were in the Krause name when she came over. She must have been connected in some way.”

I shouldn’t have been surprised, but I was. “That was fast. You got all that in just a few minutes?”

“Well there was a file on her. That was just the cover sheet info. I will get whatever else there is and pass it along as it comes.”

I didn’t ask where the file was, or what file. I was just pleased that I had a competent team. I decided to wait until Rutger called me with his info before I called him with mine.

“I am heading out to the gate now.” Kent said. “Call me on my mobile if you need me. I will do likewise if something happens.” And with that, he grabbed his jacket and was out the door.

As he was exiting, I could hear him talking with someone in the outer hall. A moment later, a guy entered the general office area and walked up to Tyler. "Are you Mr. Christian?" He asked. Tyler nodded his head in my direction.

In flawless English but with Germanic accents he said, "I am Altman Bauer. I am manager of the logistics department. Doctor Warner called me and told me to come right over and to answer any questions you may have."

■ ■ ■ ■ ■

We had seen his name in the files that Warner left us and had already matched it up to the logistics pile as someone we wanted to interview. It seemed interesting to me that Warner had arranged the interviews of the two people most likely to be involved in some way.

Bauer was a handsome and muscular young man with broad shoulders and thick, curly black hair that was slightly greying. It was combed jauntily to droop off to the side of his left eyebrow. It looked good on him and he walked with the confidence of a handsome man. He carried a satchel that seemed heavy, I guessed it was filled with work papers. I motioned for him to join me. As we walked, I saw Tasha look up and nearly faint when she saw Bauer. By then, Bauer had made eye contact with her too. It appeared to me like he was going to say something and then thought better of it.

I invited him into my office and told him to take a seat.

The only way this smuggling operation could work successfully was if the same drivers always got the routes to facilitate the illegal deliveries. That had to happen through logistics. Bauer was either involved or ignorant of someone else in his department scheduling the drivers.

I had been trained in investigative techniques and was a student and believer in Behavioral Symptom Analysis and Neuro Linguistic Programming, or NLP. These pseudo-sciences are all about interpreting how people react under duress, how to read it, control it and shape the interview accordingly.

The method of interviewing a suspect is much different than when interviewing a witness. When questioning a suspect, the approach becomes an interrogation. So, I started right in interrogating Bauer.

"Mr. Bauer, do you know why you are here?"

"Yes sir. I am here to answer any questions you may have to help you understand the logistics and shipping functions of the plant."

"No Mr. Bauer. You are here to answer my questions about smuggling and your part in those operations."

It is at this point that most innocent people protest long and loud that they are not involved. So, do guilty people. But the protests are usually completely different.

Bauer replied, "My involvement? Why do you say that I am involved?"

Bang. I knew at this point, since he was not angrily denying, he was fishing to see how much we had on him. He wasn't going to get any answers from me.

"Mr. Bauer, I need you to know that I am not the police. I am the head of security for your company. I am investigating how this smuggling is occurring so we can put an end to it and bring your friends back to work. We know you are involved ..."

Now Bauer protested. "But I am not ..."

I cut him off immediately. "Do not say a word Mr. Bauer. Not a word unless I ask you a question. Do you understand me?"

This is another point at which innocent people protest again.

Bauer said, "I am sorry. Yes, I understand."

I now had confirmation. I was only a few steps away from getting him to admit his role.

I completely changed gears and asked, "What is your relationship with Tasha Krause?"

"Tasha? What makes you think I have a

relationship with Tasha?"

This was working out perfectly. His answers phrased as questions continued to reinforce his complicity.

"Bauer, answer my question and answer it honestly." I knew he had seen Tasha out there with Peter and had seen that she was distraught. I was banking on his assumption that she had spilled the beans, if she had any to spill.

"Tell me about your relationship with Tasha."

"Tasha and I are just very good friends. Maybe a while back we had a relationship. But you have to believe me, now we are just good friends."

There it was.

With that statement he changed his position in his chair. He went from sitting with his arms folded across his chest to a long stretch with his feet creating a bridge between him and me. His hands fell folded into his lap, as if protecting himself from injury. These gross body movements are usually indicators that we were not quite at the point of him being completely honest, and I told him so.

"Bauer, I know you have told me a personal secret. But you and I both know you haven't told me the entire truth. Now try it again, and this time be honest with me."

"I am a married man, Mr. Christian. I do not need to complicate my marriage with a long-term relationship. Tasha and I met for a while. She is single, young, and as you can see, she is very pretty. We interacted at work for a while and then she asked me to meet her at her apartment to unload a heavy box from her car. I agreed, thinking nothing of it. Once I had the box in her apartment. We had a drink. One thing led to another and we had sex. It was very good for me and I could not stop seeing her. She seemed very okay with it also. After a few months we both agreed to stop."

Bauer was hoping, by making a personal admission of high risk, that I would be satisfied. He had made an admission that linked him and her, but it was not the admission I needed, or frankly cared about. I needed more, and the door was open.

"Bauer, I am not your confessor and I am not your wife. We know that you have had, and are likely still having, a relationship with Tasha. Whether or not you stop is up to you." I paused to gauge his reaction.

He just sat listening – confirmation that he was still seeing her.

"We are interested in another kind of relationship you have with Tasha. This is a business relationship I am asking about, Bauer, the side business."

He started to protest, and I cut him off, and again he did not object.

"Let me tell you how this is going to work, Mr. Bauer. When my investigation is over, the executives in New Jersey and the law departments in Paris and London are going to ask me what to do about the employees involved. Now, I am not going to try to ruin anyone out of spite, but it goes like this. They will ask me if employees were resistive or obstructive, or if they were cooperative. They are going to ask me if I think anyone needs to be prosecuted for federal crimes. You see the corporation is the complainant in those cases. They will ask me if anyone needs to be made an example of so others in the company are dissuaded from committing like acts. Do you see where I am going with this Mr. Bauer?"

Bauer could see his denials were not going to get him anywhere. And he could see that his job was at risk and worse. He could face Federal criminal charges. I continued to make the consequences for lying to me greater than the consequences of telling me the truth. He was hanging on my every word, looking for a way out. He gave it his last shot, as I knew he would.

"Yes, but I have not …"

"Bauer! Stop! You can no longer deny what

you have done. It is time for you to clear your conscience and make sure that you have a way to take care of your wife and family when this is all over."

"Can I save my job?" He asked.

There it was. His face and eyes were showing so much. He was wondering if we had anything, wondering of Tasha had ratted him out, wondering if our investigation had led to the drivers who were already talking. And he was now hoping there was a way to save his job, and more so, to avoid criminal prosecution.

I scooted my chair closer to him, our knees were almost touching. I touched his wrist lightly and said, "I can make no promises Mr. Bauer, but I can pass along that you were honest and open, that you were apologetic, if you are."

"Yes, I am sorry." He said.

Done. Now all I had to do was wrap up the details.

"There is a gentleman outside, Mr. Bauer. His name is Tyler. He will take a statement from you. I want you to give as much detail as you can remember including names of employees, dates of deliveries and how you reach the drivers and who they are. I want to know how the loads are picked up, how they get into our crates, how you got the drivers to help you, and where the goods are stored before they get onto the trucks.

"And Bauer, I also want to know step by step how Tasha is involved. And it is important that you are as brutally honest with us as she has been. If your stories do not line up, there will be a problem. Do I make myself clear? I want to know everything. Everything. Do you hear me?"

"You can refer to your notes in your satchel or to records on your computer. But I want it all. If we find you omitted anything, I think that will be perceived as resistance and deception. And that will not help you at all. Yes?"

"Yes. I understand." His head was dropping so low, his eyebrows were almost touching his knees. And I moved in for the final blow. I was in uncertain waters with this one.

"And Bauer, I want to know where all the guns are. All of them."

"Yes." Was all he said.

I left him sitting there and went out to brief Tyler.

■ ■ ■ ■ ■

Anatoly recognized the voice. They hadn't talked since Anatoly told him about the investigation and the plant closing. "Pavel my friend. How are you?"

"I have been better Anatoly, but I smile hearing your voice." Pavel and Anatoly had shared intelligence, Stasi and GRU operations in East Germany. They had drank together, gotten drunk and gotten laid together. But Pavel was a smart and ambitious man with connections, Anatoly was not. He was lucky his friend brought him along, but unless he needed something Pavel always kept him at arms length. For them to call each other friends was an expression from days gone by.

"Yes, Pavel it is good to hear from you. But enough of the bullshit. The plant is still closed, and I presume their investigation continues. Are they on to me?"

Pavel could sense the resentment in Anatoly's voice, that ingrate. So much for pleasantries between long time friends. Ever since Tasha's cousin fled, Pavel had to get the guns from Plau am See back to Reinbeck, the opposite direction of where he wanted them, and then on to Rostock and Warnemunde. It was working but was not a clean operation. It had too many steps, and too many people. He knew that complicated processes increased the risk of discovery because there were too many loose ends. And Pavel hated loose ends. Now they were under scrutiny by the German government. Pavel knew he had to come up with a better strategy but first he had to get these guns from the dock to his customers. And keeping Anatoly comfortable was part of the plan, at least for now.

"Yes, Toly. The plant is closed. We do not believe they have any idea at all who is involved. My contact says an investigator has been brought over from the States but has no idea who you are. The investigator does not speak German and will likely not be there but a few days. If we sense he is getting too close, I know where he is staying, and you can take care of him. The works-union has advised the employees not to talk with anyone, whether they know or merely suspect what is going on. And that German prick who runs the plant has no clue. The Federal investigation has stalled. They have no resources, no named suspects and their team has been disbanded. Closing the plant seemed like a final effort to extort admissions from our people and that has blown up in their faces. We believe the prosecutor and his investigator are grasping at straws at this point. Their careers are likely over."

"Anatoly, I know you may think this is going to sound like more bad news. But regardless of what you think I must still get the guns to our buyers. There is no exception. There is a shipment on the docks at the plant. It was stranded there when the plant was closed last week. It is already crated and labeled with paperwork to get the deliveries to Rostock. The fucking Poles can have the cigarettes and take them to Szczecin. It doesn't matter. Once I get this load off the docks and into your hands, I can figure an alternate way to move the guns. But this shipment has to get there."

"So, Pavel, why do you tell me this?" Anatoly asked. "What does this have to do with me? Get those god damned Poles to bring me the load in Rostock. I can handle my end. And when you figure out the next delivery schedule keep the Poles out of it. I hate working with them."

"Toly, the Poles do not work for me. They are merely part of the process. But you work for me. I have a plan and it requires your involvement. I have someone on the gates right now to let you in. He will be there all night. Get your truck and get down there. The plant is empty, the shipping door is unlocked, the crates have been dropped right by the dock door. The paperwork is already on them and in order. There is a forklift right there at the staging area. Load your truck and leave. My people will lock up after you and no one will know you have been there."

"Tonight? Pavel, it will take me at least two or three hours to get there if I drive straight through. I have never been there before and only recently met the Pole and German from the plant. This is no good Pavel."

"Anatoly. You wish to make my plans for me? This is not open for debate. The gate has our man on it and he will be there when you get there. No one is on the property. I need this and I need it done tonight. Now get ahold of Gennady and get going. Call me when you get the crates to our Warnemunde warehouse."

Pavel changed his tone and almost whispered, "Do this Anatoly, so you can be a part of the new plan. It would make me sad to think you will not be able to enjoy the continuing benefits of our friendship."

Anatoly could hear the deadly threat in the sugary words from his old friend. But he knew the expression *"Druz'ya—eto druz'ya, a biznes—eto biznes". Friends are friends and business is business.*

"Yes, Pavel. I understand. I will call Gennady and we will be on our way."

"Good, my friend. Excellent! I also have a bonus for you. Feel free to call your Polish friends and tell them you made the pickup and that you have their crates for them. Meet them in Rostock. Then kill them. They are loose ends."

Anatoly was beginning to feel like a loose end himself.

Chapter Twelve

PETER WAS A THOROUGH AND DETAIL-oriented guy. His notes and the written statement he prepared for Tasha's signature demonstrated that. His summaries were written in a precise hand and his marginalia jottings linked random comments, so several points tied together in complete thoughts. His personal notes also suggested he picked up on the fact that Bauer and Krause were still having sex, if not involved in a more personal relationship.

I was re-reading his statements from Tasha, and Tyler's from Altman Bauer. Tasha's memory must have suddenly improved because her statement took on more clarity and detail when she saw Bauer walk in. I guessed that Peter played her equally as well into cooperating honestly with the investigation. I am thinking he made some reference to her having to go back to Russia, branded as an informant, if she didn't come clean.

Tasha and Bauer's statements dovetailed.

When this all started, a long-time friend named Pavel, would notify Tasha that the guns were going to be shipped to the siding behind a small warehouse in Plau am See. There they would be stored and watched by her cousin. When the time came, Pavel would make arrangements for her cousin to move the guns to the rail siding where Pavel would rail ship them to Warnemunde. Although she said Pavel was a friend of hers from years ago, Tasha would offer no details other than his first name. She seemed almost afraid of him, even though she hinted at an earlier affair. She originally claimed not to know how Pavel got the guns or how they got to the plant.

After several go-rounds with Peter, she described how her cousin became drug addicted and of no value, and how Pavel ended up in Russia and unable to oversee the shipments to Warnemunde. Tasha then went on to explain her affair with Bauer.

It began slowly at their workplace. She portrayed Bauer as rakishly handsome and she was nearly randy, not having had sex with Pavel in ages. Her sexual connection with Altman

Bauer was almost immediate. They had sex in vacant areas of the warehouse and in his van in the parking lot. They returned to work smelling of sex and didn't care. But that was not enough. They moved their affair to her apartment. Since he was married and had no private place of his own, her place was ideal. She then described how they began going away for short weekends at her aunt's place in Plau am See.

Tasha explained how Bauer's liquor and cigarette smuggling operation was originally revealed to her in a bedroom conversation when they were making love at her apartment. He told her there were a couple guys in the plant who were smuggling stolen cigarettes and liquor into Szczecin. When she asked how that was possible, Altman said it was simple. They simply masked their delivery in an extra shipping crate. It was Altman who provided shipping and customs paperwork for the deliveries into Poland. For that he got a few extra marks a week.

Although his details were sketchy at first, a plan began to emerge for Tasha to help Pavel out of his dilemma. No matter how far she was from Pavel, she still felt connected to him. At every sex session she would tell Altman how amazed she was at his cunning, as she slowly pried the details from him. She laughed when she described Altman Bauer as “hopelessly in love” with her and blind to her manipulations. It was obvious that she had used her young body and his need for sex as a pathway to her own ambitions and, of course, her own satisfaction. “He was like a sweet little puppy,” she said. Willing to do anything she suggested, in bed or out. She had him trained and Tasha loved it.

Tasha explained that when she told her friend Pavel about it, he expanded on the idea and commanded Tasha take on the guns as well.

Tasha finally admitted to Peter that she and Pavel had been former lovers and that she longed for Pavel’s rough passion. She said, “Much like his sex, when it came to business, Pavel was demanding and quite intimidating.”

Tasha and Bauer devised a way to add one more crate – Pavel’s. The Poles were told to find a dock at Rostock as an additional stop along the way for the special crate. She said the Poles were resistant at first because it complicated their simple route. But Bauer threatened them, saying he would no longer provide them their customs paperwork. The smugglers did not want Bauer to stop providing the false shipping documents, because doing so would make their route too risky so they capitulated.

After a few more visits to Plau am See,

Tasha showed Bauer where the guns were stored in the abandoned warehouse. She explained the logistics dilemma she was having in helping a friend get the guns out of Germany. By then, Bauer was so addicted to her sexual passion he would do anything she wanted. Pavel was almost ecstatic with the arrangement to have his goods moving again. But secretly began plotting Bauer's demise. Too many loose ends.

When Pavel's buyer was ready, he would call Tasha instructing that the munitions be driven to the plant to be crated. Bauer handled that. He would drive out to Plau am See and load the correct boxes into his company truck and bring it to the plant. He would see that the right crew would crate the sealed boxes and load that crate onto a company truck. Tasha and Bauer would make sure that the crate would be affixed with the appropriate shipping papers, claiming they were automotive parts from our plant. Bauer had no idea that he was working for Pavel.

A major difference in this new arrangement was that Pavel's crates no longer went directly to Warnemunde from Plau am See. In order to get them moving again, they had to go to the plant, then on to the Poles warehouse in Rostock. There they were reloaded onto another truck and delivered to Warnemunde. There was always a crate or two of cigarettes and liquor that went on these deliveries. Those crates were also driven to Rostock where they were off-loaded into the Poles' warehouse up there.

Tasha originally claimed to have no knowledge of where the booze and smokes came from or how they got out of the country or where they went. Then she explained how they were moved.

Tasha would generate a false customer order for parts from finished goods inventory. The customers were always situated along the route to Rostock or to Szczecin. When the order was complete, she would be notified it was ready for shipment. She would then call Bauer who would notify the drivers. He saw to it that the forged shipping documents were attached to the right crates. He would then order a forklift operator to stage the real delivery of brake parts in the yard. Then, Tasha would cancel the real customer order and return the parts to inventory. This avoided any losses from being discovered and kept the customer from receiving a bill for parts they did not order.

Tasha said that initially it was fun and sexy to be a part of something this dangerous. Bauer said the Poles likely never knew they were hauling guns, just an additional load. But Tasha and he knew. And the additional money that Pavel provided was enough to change their lifestyles significantly for the better. Bauer was being paid on both ends – for paperwork and routes to cover the cigarettes and liquor, and by Pavel for his role in facilitating the movement of the guns.

Altman Bauer's story was nearly identical to Tasha's. He identified Tadeusz and Ulrich as the drivers who were running cigarettes and booze to Poland. At first, he denied involvement, but changed his story when he was convinced that Tasha had ratted him out. He too was looking to soften the blow and possibly avoid prosecution. He said he regretted ever telling Tasha about his knowledge of the smuggling operation, but he was bolstering his image during pillow talk after a lunchtime quickie. A short time later, Tasha told him a friend would pay big money to them if they could move one more crate and drop it in Rostock with clean shipping papers. He said Tasha could be very convincing when she was naked.

The excitement, the danger and the lure of additional cash made the offer too good to refuse. When Altman agreed, Tasha and he celebrated with a full afternoon of sex, not returning to work. They had been shipping the extra crates once a week to Rostock for about five months now.

Tadeusz had apparently once complained to Bauer about Russians being involved. But by then Bauer felt it was too late to back out. Besides, Tasha worried him with hints that her contact had an unsavory background.

Bauer claimed he wanted to quit, but was too frightened to say so to Tasha, for fear the Russians may find out. He also admitted that he did not want to disappoint her and end the relationship. So, there it was. He was still having an affair with her. Once he spilled his story on the smuggling of guns, he must have felt it necessary to come clean across the board. Well done, Altman Bauer.

Bauer also confirmed that the delivery on the dock right now was a “hot” load. It was left abandoned there when the police closed the plant. He felt it could have stayed safely there until the plant re-opened, since for all intent and purposes it appeared to be a legitimate order. Had we not intervened, he would have likely shipped it as scheduled, since the plan was pretty much foolproof.

Almost foolproof.

As I was reading, Tyler and Kent came back into the office. “Our guys are here and in place. They have two vans. They are parked north and south of the gate. Nothing can enter or leave without us seeing them. If there is activity, they will call me." With that Tyler lifted his mobile phone for affirmation.

"If they call, I want you to get down to the shipping docks as fast as you can and try to visually confirm what is going on in there," I replied.

"Peter and Kent will handle that. We already have vantage points inside and out of the warehouse and the gate. I will remain here and act as a command center of sorts." Again, I realized why I relied so much on Morgan Andercott's people. Anticipation and action, a recipe for success.

"And I have more news about our friend Tasha and her friend Pavel," said Kent.

Peter leaned in. I am sure he had his suspicions about his interview subject and wondered if his assumptions were right.

"Not only was our Miss Krause formerly known as Boryenko, but she was associated with a character named Pavel Oveshkin. She was his translator and girlfriend in Berlin while she was just a kid in college. Little Miss Tasha seems to get around. Oveshkin, fifteen years older than Tasha, was a mid-level officer for the armory in East Berlin. After the wall came down, he was tasked with providing the only inventory of the Armory. His report was so comprehensive and logically presented, they made him responsible for ensuring its disposition to the old Armory in St. Petersburg. There were no nukes, thank God. But there were plenty of Makarovs and Kalashnikov AK-47s and tons of ammo to go with. It was said they could arm all the border garrisons twice over from that one armory. Rumor had it that the inventory was under-reported and Pavel made his millions slowly smuggling the weapons to buyers in the Russian mafia. The guns followed roughly the same path then as now, through Rostock then aboard ship to St. Petersburg."

"I would have to see that to believe it," I said. "Moscow seems the more likely destination, given the fast uprising of the mafia there. No one knows where Oveshkin's Russian stash is, or if there are weapons left at all. But if the rumors are true, that guns are involved, then it only makes sense that Tasha would be the link. Boys, I think we are onto something here."

The three of them were smiling as if the news generated memories of the good old days. "Bad guys, guns and girls. Let's hope something pops while we are in a position to do something about it." Tyler said.

I was concerned that we may encounter something larger than we could handle if we didn't involve Rutger and his guys. But I also didn't want to be cut out of the investigation at this stage either. I decided that my team, small as it was, was fully capable. And we seemed to have plenty of backup resources in some nearby locale if we needed them. Later I would have to ask Morgan how that worked. Or maybe I didn't want to know.

I poured us each a cup of coffee and set them on the conference table, motioning for the guys to sit. I gathered them in close. "Okay, here's the deal. We hold off on sharing this new information until morning. Rutger and his boss will ask too many questions if we show them you have access to this kind of background this quickly. No sense making problems for ourselves where there aren't any. We have a surveillance crew on the gate and we can safely assume neither Altman nor Tasha are going to blow the whistle on us, since they would also be blowing the whistle on themselves."

"They won't be sharing." Peter interjected. "I explained that any deals or goodwill they may have earned will be off the table if they talk with anyone about their admissions. Indeed, word could get out immediately that they were acting as informants if they betrayed our confidence. They seemed grateful for the chance to come clean and maybe save themselves. And frankly, they seemed frightened that Pavel or Tadeusz might find out."

"Fine, let's go under the assumption we aren't blown. Also, the bad guys don't know we have the surveillance up, and that we have connected the dots with the load on the docks. With that cop out there, we can be pretty sure something is happening tonight. Am I missing anything?"

"I don't know that we have missed anything, but I sure would like to know who that polizei motorcycle cop is. Have we heard anything back from Rutger yet? Should I give him a call?" Tyler asked.

"Not yet. Let's wait him out. He too may be making connections on his end and trying to figure out what we need to know or not. I just hope we don't step on each other at some crucial moment. Let's take this one down on our own. Are you guys protected in case something goes down hard? We could be dealing with some mafia types."

Peter responded. "I think we are okay in that regard." The guys nodded and didn't offer to share more. And I didn't ask.

"Okay then. Let's grab some coffee in travel-cups, some sweets and get outside where we are better able to maneuver if we have to. It could be a long night."

As I grabbed my coat, I looked out the window. It was dark already. I had been up, without any meaningful sleep over forty hours. I couldn't allow myself to slow down or I would just crash. I pushed the files into neat piles on Warner's desk and locked the door behind me, taking only our notes and the statements from our two key witnesses.

The investigation was coming together like pieces floating in space and aligning with each other quite nicely. The question was not if they would join together, but when. And given this new cast of characters, could we assemble it without anyone getting killed? It was like putting together a puzzle with all the pieces upside down. You hoped you had all the pieces. If they all fit together, you knew when you were done. But you had no clue what it would look like until you flipped it over.

■ ■ ■ ■ ■

Gennady was still half drunk and in a foul mood. This was supposed to be his private time and he was doing as he always did. He had taken his cash payment from his last delivery and made straight for his favorite bar in the same building as his apartment room. It was a dark, seedy place in the stevedore's district. People didn't mind if you sat at a table in the back and brooded. In fact, the customers preferred Gennady stayed out of the way. It suited him just fine too.

Every now and then a hardened and well-worn girl would approach Gennady. Sometimes he was interested, as he was tonight. They proceeded to his room above the bar. It was a small place he rented by the month. The carpet was worn threadbare and would never be replaced by the landlord. He was responsible for cleaning his own bed linens, not something he cared about. The toilet and common shower were down the hall and it was a good thing too. The toilets rarely flushed all the way, and the shower floor was a mess.

So, when his phone vibrated, and he saw it was Anatoly, he cursed. He told the girl to get off him, and when she playfully hesitated, he knocked her to the floor. Anatoly's orders were hard to understand at first, something about a delivery from the closed plant. But they were to meet at the Rostock warehouse in a half hour. He rose from the bed, still inebriated and not finished with his girl. He dressed and left her on the floor. Paid, but unsatisfied.

The only thing good about being interrupted was the one thing he understood clearly. He was going to get to kill Tobiaz tonight, that disgusting, whining Pole.

■ ■ ■ ■ ■

Anatoly was supposed to be waiting for Gennady but when he pulled his beat up Lada into the warehouse parking lot, Gennady wasn't sure Anatoly was even there. The building was completely dark and there was no vehicle in the lot, but when he tried the door, it opened. Anatoly was sitting at a folding card table on an old, aluminum chair. On the table sat a battery-operated lantern on low light.

"I got a call from Pavel. There are two crates for us on the shipping dock in Reinbeck."

"But what has that to do with us Anatoly? We do not go to Reinbeck. Let that prick Tobiaz pick it up and bring it to us. It is so much safer and that is the deal. And when he gets here, I can take care of him."

"The deal is off, Gennady. Pavel wants the guns tonight. The police have closed the plant and it is empty. Pavel has a man at the gate to let us in. He said the dock door is unlocked and there is a forklift there for us. All we have to do is get the damned load and leave. No guards, no dicking with Tobiaz. But I have called him to meet us for his crate of cigarettes and booze. At first, he wanted no part of it. Did not want us to go to the plant, but also, he wanted no part of going there either. The bastard wants the reward, but none of the risk. However, the *pshek* is greedy. He will meet us here when we call. Then he is yours Gennady. So are his cigarettes and liquor."

"Then let us go Anatoly. It seems like this is the last run and I want to get it over with. I especially look forward to Tobiaz. I think I will make him suffer a bit, eh Anatoly? Like the old days."

"He is yours Gennady, however you want to deal with him. I will not be there for your private party. I will be working with a crew who will be moving the crate by boat as soon as we arrive. When we leave this place the cigarettes, liquor and Tobiaz are all yours. "And as far as this being the last run, my friend, Pavel assures me we will be a part of any new arrangements, if you still want in."

Anatoly looked at his friend forlornly. He was afraid that Pavel would see Gennady as a loose end that needed to be taken care of as well. And that task would no doubt fall to Anatoly.

Anatoly pulled the chains that opened the overhead door then jumped behind the wheel of his truck. He turned on the heater and drove down the ramp and outside the warehouse, the muffler of the big box truck spewing poisonous fumes into the frigid night air. Gennady followed and closed the overhead. He locked the pedestrian door as he walked out. They would be in Reinbeck in a few short hours, and if all went well, they would be through with this errand before daybreak.

■ ■ ■ ■ ■

Tobiaz had been caught off guard by his last call from Anatoly and had difficulty explaining it to himself. How could Anatoly have known about the crates on the dock at the plant? Tadeusz would not have told Anatoly. His cousin hated and feared the Russian. But Tadeusz had also not told Tobiaz that the crates had been picked up, so he must not have known. Besides, Anatoly had too much detail to be making it up. As much as it didn't make sense, Tobiaz had to believe Anatoly. How had the Russians gotten to a position of such power and knowledge so fast? How could they get inside the plant when even Tadeusz and Ulrich couldn't get inside their own plant?

Tobiaz was beginning to believe his worst fear was true. They were part of a gun smuggling enterprise that involved the Russians. *Matga Boga,* Mother of God. How did this get away from him?

To make matters worse, Karol's wife had not heard from her husband in over two days. It was unlike Karol to take his pay and go out on the town and not return. He was a family man and not prone to wild escapades. And Tobiaz's sister-in-law was calling daily, in a frenzy over Karol. She wanted to go to the police, but Tobiaz had so far talked her out of it. He would be unable to contain her much longer. He would need a cover story the moment she told the police Karol was with him when last seen. How could he tell the police about the Russians without implicating himself? He could not come up with an alibi and his mind was paralyzed with worry and panic. But the fact was the Russians not only involved, they seemed in charge now. He just hoped they hadn't killed Karol. They had worked out a deal. What could be so important that they would need to kill Karol?

He also couldn't explain to himself, much less to his wife, why he was now less than an hour from Warnemunde at two-thirty in the morning.

Chapter Thirteen

TYLER AND I SAT IN THE FRONT OF THE Mercedes, Peter and Kent in the back. Rutger had called and I was briefing the guys.

"The cop's name is Burke Weber. He has been with the Stadtpolizei about eleven years. His career is unremarkable, but with no demerits. He transferred from Berlin to Frankfurt, which is unusual. Even more so was his request to transfer to Reinbeck, which he described as for family reasons. Maybe so. But here he is. It seems odd to me that his path and Tasha's are nearly the same, just at different intervals. Weber requested and was transferred to the motorcycle traffic unit about two years ago. He seems clean, but we know something is up. He is supposed to be off duty, but he requested and received permission to pull an extra shift tonight. Rutger has agreed to leave him in place while we monitor his activities. I guess that is a testament to you boys. His confidence level is high. Thanks. We may have to tail Weber if he goes with the load, supposing it goes down tonight. All Rutger asks is that we report any activity related to the smuggling operation as it occurs."

Tyler looked at his guys then at me. He merely nodded, as if to say, "all in a day's work."

"Tyler, if the cop goes one way and the load another, I want us and one car to go with the load. The other unit follows the cop. Okay?"

Tyler picked up a radio from his bag and clicked the transmit button. "One to Two. Come in."

"Two here," came the response.

"Two, if the cop leaves in a different direction than the load, you take the cop and follow him to his unit barn or wherever else he goes. Keep me posted when he docks. If he meets anyone, I want photos. Over."

"Roger that One. Follow, photo, report. Out."

"One to Three. Come in."

"Three here, over."

"Three, if the cargo moves you take the lead eye on it, but not too close. We only get this one chance at it. We will follow about a half-mile behind. Keep us informed when you get to any crazy intersections where the driver may try to dust a tail to see if he is being followed. We will close the gap and take your place or cover the alternate route."

"Roger that, One. Take the eye, keep radio contact." They were speaking a language I understood from my days on the Detroit Police Department working in the Organized Crime Task Force. The *eye* is a term applied to the surveillance vehicle with the direct view of the target vehicle.

"Do your guys know that we might be dealing with some mafia types or some other kind of muscle?"

"Yes, Mike. We have that covered. They have been briefed and we can handle just about anything that might come up."

"Including armed thugs, Tyler? I don't want any of our guys getting hurt."

"Yes, we have that covered." Again, Tyler offered me no further explanation. I had plausible deniability and he was making sure of it. This was not his first rodeo.

"Okay, and if this thing looks like it is going south, or we might lose the cargo, lets take them down and hold them for Rutger and his crew."

Tyler smiled and nodded. I think he was hoping I would say that. And I think he was secretly hoping this thing would require them to intervene. I got the sense they were all thinking the same thing.

We had been sitting a few hours, exiting the vehicle only to leave some used coffee in the snow behind the car. The interior dome lights had been turned off, so we remained in the darkness. There was no more conversation, no story telling or reminiscing. This was the slow, boring, and mundane side to surveillance. It was quiet waiting, plain and simple. Unglamorous and tedious waiting. God, I wanted to go to sleep.

About one o'clock in the morning, the radio crackled.

"Two to One. We have a white box truck slowly cruising by the front gate. They did not stop."

"Two, keep an eye out. If he turns around and heads back toward the gate let me know."

"Roger that One."

I had Tyler drive us to the rear entrance of the warehouse where we had unlocked a perimeter door. We could get inside without anyone seeing us and use the loft offices upstairs for a clear view of the dock loading area.

"Three to One. The truck drove past our line of sight and has returned. It is heading back towards the gate."

"Roger that Three."

It was time. As we exited the truck Tyler, Kent and Peter grabbed backpacks from the rear and we entered the warehouse. Only the lights over the doors were illuminated. It was still very dark. We were going to have trouble making out anyone's faces in there.

As we settled in along the loft railing, Tyler plugged a combination ear bud and mouthpiece into the radio. "One to all units." He whispered. "Once the truck enters the gates, maintain radio silence. If the cop leaves, take him, but don't call it out until I clear radio silence." Both units answered affirmatively.

"Two to One, over."

"Go ahead Two."

"The cop has pulled the truck over. The driver has exited, and they are talking. They seem to be okay with each other, no defensive posturing. He does not have his hand on his gun and they are talking casually. Looks like they are finishing. The driver is getting back in the truck and the cop is opening the gate. I think this is it boys."

"Roger that Two. All units maintain radio silence."

I had to admit to a bit of excitement. It always happens before a bust, but these guys looked as cool as could be. They were as calm as if they were watching a commercial between the innings of a boring baseball game. I mentioned the low light conditions to Tyler. He smiled again and reached into his bag and hauled out a Nikon 35mm camera with a telephoto lens. It had a stick tripod for the extended lens to limit motion shake. I was familiar with this surveillance camera model.

Then he touched his fingertip to the end of the camera mount and whispered, “Infrared lens.”

That explained it. He would be seeing in the dark regardless. And they would not see the red lens disk.

I couldn't hear the sound of the door opening, but soon a stocky figure entered the pedestrian door and walked straight to the loading bay with the crates. He pushed the button for the overhead door and it opened noisily. As it rose we could see the truck had already backed into position with its rear door open, exhaust streaming upward and away in the breeze. The idling truck’s taillights painted the engine fog a blood red. The bay was perfectly chosen for a box truck, the tailgate and the dock sill aligned perfectly.

The driver soon emerged through the pedestrian door and, without hesitation, walked to the forklift. He hopped up onto the lift and started the engine, which told me the key had been left in it. He was no novice to this kind of equipment. He deftly maneuvered the forks under the first crate, lifted it a few inches and drove it straight into the truck. He settled the forks gently before withdrawing them from the skid. He did the same with the second crate. It was all over in less than three minutes.

The lift operator jumped off the lift and walked briskly to the door. His mate stood by the overhead door button. As soon as the truck cleared the dock sill by a few inches, the overhead was lowered. Before it clanked to the floor, the second man was out the door. Very efficient. Thank goodness Tyler had the camera out and focused. He cranked off a series of shots, with the dampened film motor barely making a sound. Against the sound of the forklift, the camera was indiscernible.

"One to all units. They have loaded the cargo and they are moving out. Let's get ready."

Again, terse simple responses, "Roger."

"Two to One, over."

"Go ahead Two."

"The truck has pulled through the gate and the officer is closing it. The driver of Box One has turned east onto Hamburger Strasse."

"Okay, One. You take the box truck. Two, if

the cop goes with the truck, you follow as well. If the cop goes off alone, you take the cop. We are heading to our car now."

The moment we exited the building we broke into a run to our car in the back. We were rolling toward the front gate, which would require us to drive around the monstrous grounds to catch up. I realized it was an oversight on my part.

Suddenly Tyler took a hard right through the parts storage yard and headed for a chain link gate that had been locked and closed on our earlier walk through. As we approached, Peter jumped from the car and ran to the gate, pushing it open. "I took the liberty of unlocking it earlier today when I positioned our surveillance crew. Just in case…"

This was not only going to cut minutes off our pursuit but would put us literally right on their tails.

"Two to One, over."

"Go ahead, Two."

"The cop drove off west on Hamburger Strasse and at a nice slow pace. He seems unaware we are here. We have the eye on him and will take him to bed." I knew that expression too. It meant follow him until he went home.

I was using a flashlight to study the unfolded map in my lap. "Let your crew know Tyler that these guys are likely heading to somewhere in Rostock, given Oveshkin's connection. I am guessing Highway One north to west on Highway Twenty, then up Highway One-oh-three north into the industrial dock area. It is only a guess. But an informed one." He passed that along to the eye.

Tyler spoke but his gaze never left the road, "If they follow that course, it will allow us to drop back to following only their tail lights. We will switch on and off with the eye at entrance ramps, so we look like different headlight patterns in their rear-view mirror. Rostock is only about two and a half hours away, depending on how they drive."

"Given their cargo," I offered, "I am guessing they will obey the speed limits."

Sure enough, *Box One*, what we now called the white truck, entered onto Highway One north. We had a long ride ahead of us. This again was the tense but boring part. If they exited anywhere along the route, it would be a challenge to avoid being spotted while following them off the highway and then back on. This is where surveillance got tricky. It is not at all like you see on TV or in the movies.

I had some mobile calls to make. The first was to the front gate guard to tell him to lock the back gate and the dock door. He still seemed unaware that his back-gate officer was missing and seemed confused by my order. He would now know his guard was gone. I would find out in the morning what his report would look like.

It was after two in the morning. Rutger picked up on the first ring.

"This is Mike, Rutger. I want to give you an update. We actually found several crates on the dock here and they were labeled for shipment. Weber was attending the rear gate here when he admitted a truck with two men in it. They proceeded directly to the correct dock with the staged crates. They entered through an unlocked door and loaded the crates using a company forklift. They then left and are now driving north on the Autobahn One. If I am thinking correctly, they will try to make their way to Rostock. The most direct route is …"

"Yes, I know. They will get onto Twenty west just south of Rostock and then head north on One-oh-three, but how do you know where they are now? Wait. Let me guess. You are running your own surveillance."

"Rutger, I do not know how much you wish to know or when it is better for you not to know. So, let me tell you what we are doing. Stop me when you think you should."

"We have Weber under surveillance. We have a professional crew following him. If he does not suspect anything then we will follow him where he goes. If he enters the polizei stationhouse, then we will let you know immediately. In fact, you may wish to make arrangements to pick him up there, just in case. If he heads home, we will put him to bed and call you, either way.

"We also have the truck and the two guys in it under surveillance. I am currently in the second chase-car and we are intentionally a good half-mile or more behind. They are well within the speed limit and driving cautiously. I am guessing that even though they have good paperwork, they do not wish to be detained. It may make good sense to have officers available in Rostock. I am guessing they will drop the cargo for pickup at a later time." I also gave Rutger the make, model and license plate information on Box One.

"Well, you certainly have taken over, haven't you?"

"I am sorry Rutger, I did not mean …"

"No, No, Mike. It is fine. With the limited resources at my disposal, I could not have done this nearly as well, if at all. It is good. I will plan to grab Weber and I will have a tactical response crew positioned for you in Rostock. I am at least two hours out of Rostock and cannot get there by the time you do. Do not get hurt. These guys may be armed, especially if there is a Stasi-Russian connection. I do not want you or your people to be hurt trying to intervene, let my people do it. When I have the tactical team leader's info, I will have him call you directly. You can coordinate as you arrive."

Although I didn't have any law enforcement jurisdiction in Germany, I was authorized to conduct an internal company investigation. I intended to do so, to its conclusion. The only exposure we had was if my guys were armed and we got into it. There is no provision for foreign, armed-security personnel in Germany that has not been pre-approved through our respective State Departments. I had made no such arrangements. Being armed foreigners in plain clothes, our actions could be considered more than merely criminal. They might also be considered espionage if my guys were in any way still connected to their armed services units. Right now, I had plausible deniability. But if shots were exchanged, we would all be *in the stew*, so to speak.

"Makes sense to me Rutger." I switched gears on him. "What new information do you have on Tasha or Altman, anything?"

"Nothing deeper than what I gave you earlier today. But Interpol seemed very interested that we were asking for a deeper dive into our friend Pavel. He is believed to have stolen a significant cache of arms and ammo from the East Berlin Armory, but there is no proof. The Russians aren't admitting it and they have no valid inventory other than Pavel's own. Interpol is pushing some buttons to get more detail from their other member partners."

I was guessing the other member partner was the Russians. Good luck with that.

"Okay, Rutger, I am guessing we are about an hour outside of Rostock. I will await your team leader's call. Let me know if you get anything more on Krause or Oveshkin." We made our good byes and disconnected our call.

Tyler spoke up first. "I hope we don't have too many chefs in the kitchen when we get there. It could get hectic. And I sure don't want to be the victim of friendly fire, especially in a civilian situation. It may make sense for us to talk about the rules of engagement. How do you want us to handle a take down, if necessary?"

I had been planning for this question. "I've given it some thought. But let me ask you a couple questions first. You have hinted that you have covered the contingency that these guys may be armed. I am not so worried about a civil suit if something goes awry. We have attorneys for that. I am more worried about the diplomatic and criminal charges that may come if you have to use weapons, which I assume you have in your little bag of tricks in the back."

"I am not concerned that you don't know what you are doing. To the contrary, I believe you can handle anything that comes our way. I am concerned however that even if we act correctly, once we bust a few caps, we are prima-facia breaking German law. I don't want to get jammed up and don't want you guys locked up either. My company will take care of me, but it is a lot for Morgan to take on."

"So, my first thought is this. We take these guys to their drop point and call it in to the tactical team. Then we follow them or sit on them until the cops can take them off. What do you think?"

Tyler drove a bit before answering. "I am good with that. It is safe for everyone concerned. This isn't our first time doing something like this, as I am sure you have guessed by now. And by the way, the guys and I are very comfortable working with you. You give us our lead and you make good decisions. We feel like it is a good partnership."

I was secretly pleased to hear that.

"However," he continued, "these guys we are following do not appear to be amateurs. If the intel is correct, that they are Russians and Stasi, they are trained soldiers and likely killers.

We will be armed if we get close in. Yes, we have weapons and other tactical gear in the back. I guess you have figured that out as well. These guys may be good, but if they are regular military or just street thugs, we won't even need our weapons. If they have a bit more training, we will still likely not need our weapons, but won't take any chances. Does that work for you?"

"When your confidence level is high, it seems easier to take what others consider to be *more risk*." I replied. "So, yes. I am good with that protocol. But I am also willing to let the police chase these guys down if we lose them in surveillance, or if they spot us in Rostock and bolt. I do not want innocent civilians getting hurt if we get solely involved in what should be a police action. But I also agree, these guys may be bad actors. Do not allow your team to get hurt."

"Nor you, Mike. When we arm up, we have gear for you too."

"Thanks Tyler. Let your guys know the rules."

He spent the next several minutes explaining the rules of engagement, nearly verbatim, to the crew of the eye.

My private thought was that I was not *arming up*. I had no intention of going to jail if I had to use a weapon. It would be better for me to stay out of the way and avoid the need all together. I was staying in my capacity as private citizen and corporate security guy. That's it. I hired these guys to take the risks. My rules of engagement were designed to be on record as minimizing any risk. Even to the point of losing these bad guys right at the end. God, I hope it didn't come to that.

▪ ▪ ▪ ▪ ▪

Gennady wanted to wait in the truck and watch for the boat. It would be much warmer. But Anatoly insisted they park it inside. He did not want the police, or anyone else for that matter, to question a vehicle parked alongside an empty warehouse in the port town of Warnemunde. So, while Anatoly sat inside with the lantern and the space heater, he sat outside behind a dumpster and rolled his collar further up over his neck, taking shelter from a brisk northerly breeze as he waited for the boat. The chill air blew straight at him off this bay in the lower Baltic Sea and continued southward to Rostock a few miles away. The trawler was following the same path as the cold winter wind, possibly even being driven by it. He hoped it would arrive soon so he could get back inside. The thought of being out here in the dark, alone and cold, depressed him.

Gennady was never what anyone would call an educated man, but he always thought he was street smart. He could spot an easy mark and take him off without any trouble at all. Sometimes his mere physical presence was so imposing that people just gave up their money without even being asked. Other times, someone would resist, either out of fear or false bravado. But Gennady wasn't merely big, he was fast, strong and military trained. He rarely even encountered a bruised knuckle. He knew he didn't have a good command of any language, even his own. He also was aware others thought him to be uneducated and a brute. He wasn't likely ever to be the brains behind any plan, but he resented being given all the dirty jobs. Drive this, pick this up, clean this, and go get this. And like tonight, go sit outside in the cold and watch. It angered him, more than he could talk about, that even his friend Anatoly treated him that way.

In fact, it was Anatoly, more than anyone else, who made him feel insignificant. Anatoly made more money on every job even though they shared all the risk. Anatoly made all the decisions, even when Gennady's life was at stake.

He knew that Anatoly could find anyone to

do his dirty work. Driving guns across the border had started out as a fun way to make some money together. They shared risk based on mutual trust. They had been equals in the service. And now this. Gennady was basically Anatoly's *podchinennyy*, his slave. The more Gennady thought about it, the deeper his brows furrowed. He felt he was looking narrowly out from a dark cave that closed in all around him. Although he had nowhere to go, Gennady knew it was time to move on. After he killed Tobiaz, he would tell Anatoly he wanted to quit.

Chapter Fourteen

I WAS ON MY MOBILE PHONE TALKING with the local Unit Leader, Lutz Reiter, of the Grenzschutzgruppe 9. It was commonly known as the GSG9, the German Special Response Team.

In 1973, the German Federal Police decided they needed to form a new, very well trained and equipped, tactical response unit. The decision was made after a world-famous, and catastrophic blunder of theirs. The German Police attempted the rescue of Jewish athletes, from the Black September PLO terrorists, at the Munich Olympic Games in 1972. Many hostages were killed in the assault to free them. Their new methods and tactics were based on those of the famous British SAS counter terrorist and Israeli Special Operations groups.

Reiter was the GSG9 guy up this way. He had been quite well briefed by Rutger and I could tell he was being polite with me. Nevertheless, he wanted me out of the way as soon as he and his guys arrived on scene, which could be in the next fifteen minutes or so. Right now, I was relegated to giving him location information and good physical descriptions of my team and myself. Reiter did not want any "unfortunate errors" and I did not want to become one.

We hung up in agreement that our team would keep the eye on the building to make sure no one left without our seeing it. As soon as Reiter came on scene, they would take over and move in for arrests. It all seemed a bit premature to me. I had hoped to see the two guys in the truck taken into custody, yes. But more than anything, I wanted to tail these guns to their destination and to bring Pavel into the net as well. Now that, to me, was a neat closure to the case.

Peter was afoot. He had taken up a position outdoors, around a corner behind the warehouse, watching for anyone approaching from the rear, dockside. He was behind an empty shipping container and had great concealment, while still having a vantage point to watch the water approach. It wasn't long before he spotted someone hiding behind a trash dumpster back there. Although it could have been a vagrant, the guy was facing out to sea. He looked more like a lookout than someone hunkering down to sleep the night away on the streets.

Peter fell back, waited and watched. Within minutes he confirmed him as a lookout when the guy lifted binoculars to his face as if scanning the horizon. He called it in.

We now had a different set of assumptions than when we got here. We were now going with the premise they were waiting for a boat to pick up the load. We had not planned on that contingency and had no way of following a watercraft. If we let the cargo get away, we would still end up with the drivers, but with no way to prove what the load was. Hopefully the GSG9 guys would get here soon and make that call. We had at least one bad guy in the warehouse and one outside, at the back corner of the building.

Our Unit One driver had parked in a lot down the street from the driveway of the warehouse. Nothing could approach that way without being spotted by our guys. He called in, "There's a white van approaching with just one occupant that we can see. We can't get a look at the license plate from here."

In just a moment, we could see it pull into view. It drove directly to the overhead door. Tyler used his telephoto lens to get a look at the plate before it backed in. The driver exited, walked up the ramp and into the man-door. He may have been here before or was just very familiar with warehouse loading docks.

As with any plan, it all goes to hell with the first engagement with the enemy. We now had to figure our alternatives. What the hell did we have? We had a guy watching out to sea, convincing us he was awaiting a boat. We had a guy at the dock with a truck and we had a guy inside.

Tyler asked, “What’s the plan?”

■ ■ ■ ■ ■

Tobiaz was furious at having to drive to Warnemunde to meet the Russians. “Okay, Anatoly. What the hell is going on? How did you get inside that closed plant? And where the hell is Karol? The last time I saw him was days ago and he was with Gennady.”

Tobiaz was tired of his questions going unanswered, especially as it pertained to his brother and this time it would be different. They would answer him or there would be hell to pay.

“Well, my Polish friend. It is good to see you too. Why so angry? Didn't I call you to come get your load? How I got in is none of your damned business. The fact that I am here, with your crates, should tell you enough. As for your brother, I do not know where he is, but if you have questions for Gennady, he is outside. Go ask him." God, Anatoly hated this Pole and would be glad when Gennady took care of him.

The last thing Tobiaz wanted was to be alone with Gennady. There was something evil about the man and he seemed only somewhat under Anatoly's control. Even so, he could not return to Szczecin without an answer for Karol's wife. He was determined to confront Gennady, no matter how frightened he was of him.

"Where outside, Anatoly? I will go ask him. And when I return, I will take my goods and go. Then we are finished. I quit."

"Yes," Anatoly smiled to himself. "You are finished indeed."

Anatoly grunted and turned his back on Tobiaz. "Go to the water side. He is there."

▪ ▪ ▪ ▪ ▪

I was mulling over Tyler's request for a plan. At this point there were several variables that had to be considered. If the newly arrived driver left with a crate, he had to be followed. That would be Team One's job from outside the warehouse gates. But it would reduce our crew to one vehicle.

We could wait for the boat. If a boat came, we would keep them all under surveillance until Reiter's team arrived to arrest them.

There was also the matter of the truck and crates inside the plant with at least the guy inside and the guy outside. We could continue to watch them. But if they left, we would have to make a fast break for the warehouse to ensure it was empty. If it was, we would follow Box One again. If the crate was inside, we had a problem. We would have to split up with a vehicle following Box One and someone staying behind to wait for the boat and Reiter's team.

Those seemed the only options right now.

Tyler didn't hesitate. He began dividing responsibilities for each contingency. It was agreed that Kent and I would stay with the crate if Box One left. Tyler, Peter and the guy from Team One would take Box One and the two guys.

It was all we had, but it covered the contingencies.

"Look," Tyler said to me. "It is time to gear up. We may have to move fast and may not have time to even get to our stuff if we have to roll right out of here. Mike, you and Peter go gear up." They were out of the car before I could even say a word. Obviously, it made sense.

Peter unzipped the first nylon bag revealing several black, form-fitting bulletproof vests. He handed me one and said put it on under my coat. He slid off his jacket and began suiting up. I figured out the Velcro straps and tightened mine down. It fit like it was made for me. This was way different than the Second Chance Vest that I wore on the Detroit Police Department when I was in the Tactical Mobile Unit. That old vest was basically filled with sand and some small-caliber, bulletproof Kevlar plates. These tonight were the real deal. They were lightweight and capable, I guessed, of resisting any small arms ammo, as long as I didn't get shot in the face.

Peter was already opening bag number two as I was cinching my straps.

Inside was what I had suspected, sort of. He handed me a Makarov 9mm in a nylon holster.

"A Makarov?" I asked.

"Lugers seemed a bit clunky," Peter replied.

I slipped it from the holster and Peter said, "Careful, it's loaded with one in the chamber."

I noticed the safety was set in the down position, so I drew the slide partially back to see the brass casing. I released the magazine then pulled back the slide to eject the chambered round into my hand. I wanted to see them for myself. It's an old habit.

Peter smiled in acknowledgement. There were twelve rounds in the magazine and one in the chamber. That should be plenty.

"The first round is a hollow point, as I am sure you noticed. The next rounds in the magazine alternate hollow and half jacked. The magazines are new, and the springs are fresh. There should be no jamming."

I popped four rounds from the magazine and looked up.

Again, Peter smiled in acknowledgement. "Yes, the alternating hollow points are cross-cut. They will open for you to about the size of a quarter as they tear through your target. Maximum efficiency."

Hmmm. I thought to myself. Maximum damage. I liked it. I did not relish the thought of a slightly wounded guy firing back at me. If I had to do any damage at all, I wanted it to be maximum.

As I slid the reloaded weapon back in the holster Peter handed me two more full magazines in a nylon-belted holster. "This ought to cover it," he said.

Thirty-seven tries to hit my target. If I missed him, maybe I could deafen him. So much for my plan to remain unarmed.

Chapter Fifteen

TOBIAZ COULD FEEL THE LIGHT BREEZE IN his face as he walked outside. The wind was sheltered along the south side of the building and almost seemed calm and quieting. If this had been a stroll along a waterside park with his wife, it would be very pleasant indeed. Normally he loved being by the water, but not tonight. The sky didn't even reflect the lights from Rostock a few miles south. The dark clouds were so dense they didn't show their definition, just stole the light and didn't give any back. As he turned to walk along the west side of the building, he could feel the wind pick up off the bay. It was cold enough to sting his pale cheeks and brought tears to his eyes. With eyes brimming, Tobiaz didn't see Gennady waiting for him, gun in hand.

"Well, well, well," Gennady said, startling Tobiaz. "Look who is here. The other whiny little Pole. The complainer. What brings you here to visit me on this cold night Tobiaz?"

Tobiaz was shocked to see Gennady so close. How did he miss him? And why was he pointing a gun at him? "Put that thing away, Gennady. I have some questions for you. Then I am gone. Out of your life forever."

Gennady, smirked at the irony of that last remark. "You are already nothing to me Tobiaz. What do you want?"

"You were the last person I know who saw my brother. Where is he?"

"Karol is dead. I shot him. I shot him in the face Tobiaz. And now you are going to join him." Gennady leveled his gun at Tobiaz's face, just as he had done to Karol.

Tobiaz heard the quiet *pffft* of a muffled shot and Gennady's head exploded as he fell to the ground. Then he heard the sound of feet running toward him but could not react in time. The last thing he remembered was a terrible pain in his head. And then it all went black for him.

"Tyler, come in. Come in." I sat straight up at the sound of urgency. We had seen the late arrival leave the building and walk back to the waterside.

"Go ahead Kent. What is it?"

"I just had to take action with extreme prejudice back here. The watcher was about to shoot a guy in the face. I took him out." The other guy is subdued and restrained with plastic ties. I had no choice. I took out the one acting like a prick."

Tyler said, "Frisk them and grab any hardware. Gag the one guy so if he wakes up, he stays quiet."

"Done and done."

"Stay back there a bit more Kent and wait on that boat. When the cops get here, we will coordinate the report."

Now I was worried. My biggest concern had been that we might have to use force. Now we had, and someone was dead for it. This was going to be tough to explain. Not impossible, but difficult. How did Kent decide who to shoot? Was it the right call? Could he have resolved it better? And how was it that I never heard the shot?

"Look Tyler, you guys are great, and your training is obviously the best. But my company and I now have exposure. And frankly, so does your whole team. I have to admit to being concerned. Hell, it is worse than that. I'm worried we're all going to jail."

"I know you're worried Mike. But we have this. Trust me. We are okay. Just stick with the plan."

■ ■ ■ ■ ■

Aleksey Lagunov looked out from the enclosed bridge of his vessel. He loved the water. He was *born to it* as they say. He grew up on the coastal shoreline of St. Petersburg and sailed from the time he was twelve. At seventeen he enlisted in the Russian Navy. When his officers and many crew-mates died in a fuel explosion aboard ship, he was given a junior level promotion. There was a joking rumor that the explosion could not have been an accident, given that nine people had to die for Aleksey to get a promotion. True or not, the only thing the promotion did for him was to develop a deep disgust for all people of rank. It separated him from what he loved, a life of hands-on sailing. But it also strained his relationships with his former peers and they came to hate him.

He became defensive, arrogant and cocky with his superiors and cruel toward those ingrates below him. At their first opportunity, the higher-ups drummed him out.

Since then he had been taking jobs as a merchant seaman and keeping busy enough to support himself. Over time, he bought a small used trawler. The vessel looked worse than it actually was and that worked to Luganov's advantage in negotiating the price. He knew the engines could easily be restored and he really wasn't worried about its looks. In less than a year, he tuned her out as a trusted working craft that slipped through the waters effortlessly. When he told his girlfriends in ports along the Baltic that he owned his own ship, they thought he might be a wealthy and generous man. That worked to his advantage too.

He loved the steady thrum of the engines in his old boat. He reveled in the rush of water across the unpainted black, metallic skin of his powerful shark. Worn and weather-beaten, she looked slow and languid, but she was uncharacteristically powerful, capable of quiet glides or fast rushes through the murky sea. Built in Kaliningrad, his Temnaya Noch', Dark Night, was twenty meters. It wasn't too big, but it served him well. In the dark seas she was almost invisible. He acquired a crew and together they maintained her engines in meticulous condition as he expertly plied her along the entire coastline from St. Petersburg to Warnemunde and beyond. His papers were clean, regardless of his work.

Pavel Oveshkin was Lagunov's best paying client. So, when Pavel called, Aleksey and his crew changed course out of Gdansk and departed for Warnemunde. The breeze was up to about ten knots, but northerly from his back. The seas rolled gently and pushed him along. He had used less fuel than he budgeted and that would save him some money on the deadhead end of the trip. It may cost him a few more rubles heading back, but he would recover them when Pavel paid him.

He could make out shore lights now and his heading showed him to be on course for his landing. Navigating back across the open water would be a bit tougher, but a three-foot swell would not bother him, his crew, or his boat. He felt he had plenty of fuel to clear out of the Warnemunde area and head back. It would take them easily to Bornholm Island, and the port at Nexo, where he could top off his tanks. He would be virtually anonymous there, except to a girlfriend or two, and there were plenty of coves to put up along the way if he had to wait for things to cool off. Aleksey loved the idea that he was a pirate. The free spiritedness, the cat and mouse, the danger and the rewards all excited him beyond words.

Now it was time to make sure his crew was ready. He would start with a review of a drawing of the dockside loading area. They had been there several times before, but he always followed the plan. They each had a role in hoisting aboard the crate and lashing it below deck. They would not have to go ashore if Gennady and Anatoly did their jobs.

Then he would make sure each of the crew checked and rechecked their weapons. The Kalashnikovs Pavel sold him at a discount were excellent weapons and reliable even in the damp sea air. Regardless, he insisted they maintain their weapons like the machinery on his boat, clean, oiled and operational. He and his crew had been involved in a few scrapes over the years and each member was perfectly reliable. These were men he could count on, in good times and in bad.

■ ■ ■ ■ ■

Kent could see the trawler lights while they were still about a mile out. The sky was calm and dark, but visibility was at least a few miles across the water. Their heading was unmistakable. They were on course to this harbor. There was nothing he could do right now with the dead body. It was somewhat concealed by the dumpster. Kent dragged the unconscious man further out of sight, hiding him between the dumpster and some stacked wooden pallets. He secured the gag then called in his sighting to Tyler.

I heard Tyler's half of the conversation and got the gist of it. We were going to have a problem if Lutz Reiter didn't get here pretty soon. It was possible we could be outmanned and outgunned depending on the size and skill of the crew. I was also concerned about bodies piling up if we had to defend ourselves. We already had broken Rutger's admonition to not intervene.

I made a decision.

"Let's get all our crew back here Tyler. That crate isn't going anywhere. We have about the time it takes to explain our plan to them, as it will take for that boat to arrive. Once that happens, we will have more people to contend with and that crate could end up on a ship to God only knows where."

"By now that guy inside has to wonder where one of the other two is. If he gets the least bit curious, he'll be on edge and expecting trouble. So, let's get the team here and I will begin the briefing over the radio."

My plan was simple in its statement.

"We go inside and convince the guy in there to surrender. Then we don't answer the door when the other guys get here. That should get them back on their boat and heading home without their payload. But if we can take them down without any gunplay, we do that and put a bow on the package for Reiter and Rutger. If it looks too dicey, then we let them go but identify the boat for further intelligence or investigation."

Tyler had a modified idea. He wanted to let the guys load the boat so that we had the evidence on their vessel. Then we take them all down.

I was a bit worried about that option because even Rutger was satisfied with just taking back the guns and letting any couriers go. If we shot anyone in the process, even in self-defense, Rutger could always go on record with Felder and say we were warned not to intervene. I wasn't comfortable with that.

"Mike," Tyler said. "Trust me. We can get right into their jackets and give them a hug and they wouldn't know we were there."

I had heard about some units with that ninja kind of skill but had never believed it. Something always went wrong. I had to give clear rules of engagement. I was afraid though that they would find a loophole. They weren't used to standing down at a prime moment.

I had to rely on their training and their good judgment.

"Okay. Here's the deal. You are absolutely not to engage these guys with weapons other than in self-defense. And you are to do everything to remain concealed except when we take down the guy inside. If the guys in the boat escape, then so be it. But no shots fired at them.

"Now Tyler, what is your plan to take the guy inside into custody without shooting him?"

"Simple, we walk right up to him and take him into custody."

I found that to be a bit light on the details and said so.

Tyler nodded to Peter. "Unit One will drive loudly into the parking area and create enough noise to attract the subject's attention. Meanwhile we will have scaled the back side of the building. We will use the distraction to come in through the roof utility hatch. We will come along the ceiling girders and rappel down. He will not even know we are there. When we get alongside him, we will invite him to surrender. We will then use the minimum force necessary to overcome any resistance. You know, a citizen's arrest."

Peter made it sound so easy, as to be ridiculous. But I could tell he was dead serious. They had a plan and it was all we had.

There was no double-checking the plan. There was no one asking for details about their role. I could hear Tyler and Kent stuffing a bag from the trunk as I watched out the front window of the van. They ran close to the ground along the blind side of the two-story building. I was guessing grappling hooks but saw none of their supplies.

Kent came onto the radio speaking low and quiet. "They are about fifteen-hundred yards out and motoring slowly. I can't even see a wake. It is a long trawler type boat with a winch. They must all be inside the bridge or quarters, because I can't see anyone outside manning lines yet."

I had no one to tell. The guys were all on assignments. So, I called Reiter.

"Mr. Christian, I hope you and your men are sitting safely away. We are still about five to ten minutes out. We have been reviewing the building prints and highway exit routes in case something goes amiss. I already have asked for a patrol vessel to back us up. This is standard protocol on any waterside assault. So, you can sit tight and keep us apprised if they head out. It would be nice if you got the boat numbers should they depart with the crate by water. Our plan will be to ensure you are safely away, then we will secure the building and call them out. It is very likely they will surrender when they realize they have nowhere to go."

My stomach was weak from knowing we had already gone way beyond "sitting it out safely." Someone was already dead, and my team was about to breach the building. Reiter hung up before I could respond.

At that moment, Unit One came screeching

into the parking lot, gunning the engine and turning circles near the loading dock. He did this two or three times before the warehouse front door opened. I couldn't get a good look at the guy, but he was wearing a short black coat, maybe leather. He stood there with something in his hand, likely a gun, but I couldn't be sure. Then Unit One just as suddenly left through the front gate and drove away. The guy in the front door hesitated. I could see him looking around. Then he slammed the door shut. Oh my God. Hopefully my guys were in that fast or they were going to be stranded on the roof. Or they lost the element of surprise and it was going to get ugly.

I waited in painful silence. Minutes passed, and nothing. The radio Tyler left me was quiet. Then I realized I had turned it off when I was talking with Reiter.

I quickly turned it on to hear Tyler, "Kent are you there? Come in Kent"

"Go ahead Tyler"

"Where is the boat Kent? How far out?"

"Less than a hundred yards out. There are two men at the rails holding coiled ropes. Obviously, one is piloting. So, we have at least three. I make them here in under two minutes."

"Okay Kent, here's the plan. Our friend isn't going to be coming out to meet these guys. At least one or two of them will have to come in and check, or they will leave after not making contact. Either way, just call it out to us. Can you see the mooring posts? Any idea where they will be tying up?"

"There are two likely berths Tyler, they are about eighty feet apart. Neither will be close to me."

"Okay Kent. That answers my question. No way to take the pilot out if he stays aboard alone. We may lose him if he flees, but our orders are to let him go, if he does."

"Mike, are you there? Come in, Mike."

"Yes, Tyler. Sorry, I had my radio off when I was talking to Reiter. Is everything okay?"

"Yes, Mike. We are fine, and we have one in custody. Exactly as planned and no shots fired. But our friend here may be reading with one eye and eating his steak through a straw for a few weeks."

God, I like working with these guys. When I grow up, I want to be just like them.

"Okay, what's the deal with the shore patrol? What's your plan?"

"We are leaving the front door unlocked. I am guessing at least one or two of them will come looking for their guys. When they get here, we will ask them to turn over their weapons and surrender. I am sure they will be fully cooperative."

"Perhaps. But I think they will be suspicious to not be greeted when they dock. Remember, there was once a lookout. I can't have any shots fired and this assault you have planned will be more dangerous than the other you just pulled off. So, here is the rule: take no chances. If you can't get them to surrender without gunplay, then do not announce yourselves. There is a patrol boat en route along with the tactical guys. In fact, they might get here before these guys get ashore. Remember, no gunplay."

"Roger that. No gunplay."

It was Kent. "They are tying up now. They are at the closest slip. I can see them clearly and hear them. They have no idea I am here, and our little friend is still asleep. They have AK47s strapped over their shoulders."

That is some heavy firepower. I had to warn them. "Guys, they are packing some serious heat. Fall back into hiding and let the GSG9 guys handle this."

I waited for a response. None.

Kent again, "Okay, they are heading alongside the building toward the front. Two of them and weapons at the ready."

I didn't give it a thought. I broke for the front door to get there ahead of them. I had to make sure the guys knew they were in for some serious firepower and to confirm they would lay off.

The sailors hadn't turned the corner when I tried the front door. As I reached for the door, it was yanked open and I was dragged inside by my collar.

"What the hell are you doing?" whispered Tyler. "Are you out of your mind? We've got this. Now get behind the truck over there and stay there."

I looked around and saw no one else in the building. "Where …?"

"Go!" he whispered.

I did so. I padded my way quickly behind the engine compartment of the truck. I don't know when it happened, but my gun was in my hand. I looked down and saw the safety was already off as well. Some instincts stay with you, I guess. I looked up and the warehouse was empty again. I feared I was the only one who might get spotted, so I laid down on the floor behind the big truck wheel and watched from the prone position.

Within seconds the front door opened, and a gun barrel protruded inside followed by its owner. The same for the second guy.

"Zdravstvuyte, Kto zdes"? Anatoly, vy zdes'?" Silence. No one was here as far as they were concerned.

I heard it at the same time they did. A

muffled sound in the far corner. They turned in the direction of the sound and missed it. I almost did too, it happened so fast. Tyler and Peter rappelled from the rafters so fast, the two sailors didn't even have time to look up. They were kicked to the ground as my guys slid to their landing. They were almost unconscious when they were both chopped on the back of the head with the butts of two 9 millimeters. It seemed nearly choreographed, it happened in such unison.

For all my worries, it was exactly as Tyler declared, "We have this."

And they did.

Tyler was already wrapping one guy's wrists in duct tape he pulled from his bag. Peter had the other guy's wrists and feet taped also. As soon as Tyler was finished, they hoisted these two over their shoulders. Like firemen, they literally ran the two hundred-pound guys over to the crate that was sitting like an altar in the middle of the empty warehouse floor. There was another unconscious figure already stretched out on the top of the crate. As I looked closer, I could see he was thoroughly taped to it. That must have been the first guy. They quickly set about fastening the last two in the same manner. It would take quite a while to cut them out of their cocoon much less for them to try to escape.

The matter of the guy on the boat was beginning to resolve itself as well. Kent called in.

"Must have been only one guy aboard. He turned off the engine and is heading your way. And he is packing heat too."

"Okay Kent. FYI, we have everyone in custody here. No injuries. Well, not to us anyway. Let us get this last one buttoned up and we can be on our way, except for that mess you have back there."

"Thanks for that. Okay, guys, he just turned the corner and is out of my line of sight."

"Take cover, quietly." Tyler ordered.

When I looked out from my vantage point behind the truck wheel again, the place was empty. How did they do that?

Slowly, an invisible hand pushed the door open. Same routine. *"Zdravstvuyte, Kto zdes'?"*

The gunman entered through the front door. This time there was no distracting sound. Tyler merely stepped from behind the door and clocked him one with the Makarov. The skipper went down like a ton of bricks.

▪ ▪ ▪ ▪ ▪

While the guys were taping him to the side of the crate, Kent called in. "Guys, we have company. A police car has pulled up in front.

Pretty bold and pretty obvious."

Before I could respond Tyler took it. "Kent, wipe your gun completely clean and don't forget the bullets and magazine. Leave it near the dead guy. Toss the silencer and your spare magazines in the bay. Peter is on his way to unlock the back door nearest your corner. Come join us. I will handle the explanation to the authorities."

To us Tyler added, "Give me all your tactical gear. All of it. Guns, ammo, vests, everything."

We quickly stripped off our vests and holsters. Tyler stuffed it into his duffel along with their rappelling gear and tape. He bolted out the back door and was back in a flash. I knew he had deep sixed it all in the harbor. He may have to go back and retrieve it later, but for now it was gone.

"Okay. We clean?" he asked. "Then let's go meet our rescuers."

I knew where he was going with this. But felt it was my place to handle the cops. I was worried about things like fingerprints and gunshot residue, and I said so as we walked to the door.

Tyler said, "We've got that covered."

And I believed him.

I called Reiter before we walked outside. I didn't know if his tactical guys were already in position or not, but I didn't want any of us to become mistakes of friendly fire. "Reiter, we are inside the warehouse. Everything is under control. We have the cargo and the suspects and there is no armed threat. I repeat, no armed threat. Can you come in, alone, first? I want to show you something."

Reiter was about to speak, and I think he wanted to take control, but I hung up before giving him the option and looked out the door. It took a moment but then I saw a large, dark-black, box-truck pull into the yard and approach the building. The black matte lettering said *Spezielle Antwort Einheit* boldly on the side – Special Response Unit. When it stopped, one man, dressed smartly in tactical gear, got out of the back. Reiter was every bit a tactical leader, muscular, lean and determined. And he didn't look happy.

I met him at the door.

"Lutz Reiter? I am Michael Christian. It is good to see you. And thank you for coming. Before we go inside, I want to bring you up to date on some developments."

"As you know, I have my own investigators helping me on our case. Becker has met them, and Herr Felder is aware of them. We conducted an internal corporate investigation that established there was a load on the dock in our empty plant waiting for drivers to smuggle it out. We really don't even know what is in the smuggled crates, but we have our suspicions.

"We set up a surveillance on our warehouse after we established that a Stadtpolizei officer named Burke Weber had taken it upon himself to replace our rear gate guard at the plant."

"Yes, Weber had been picked up and taken to our offices for interrogation." Reiter added.

"Good." I continued. "We called Rutger once we were able to confirm that the load had been moved from our warehouse dock into the truck that is now inside this warehouse. I am assuming by your prompt response he contacted you right away. We had the truck under constant surveillance until it pulled inside. Then we notified you exactly where we were."

"Meanwhile, I set up a rear spotter, given this was a dockside facility, to keep a lookout around the rear for a boat to take this load. That is when I was notified that there was a man unconscious and tied up in the back and another one dead from a gunshot wound. I had my guy back off from the scene and take cover.

"Shortly after, a boat arrived, and two men disembarked with weapons. In the meanwhile, and in order to see what was going on inside, a couple of my guys made their way onto the roof and got inside. When it appeared that the load was going to be moved, my guys made a decision to seek the surrender of the three guys inside. It worked out well and we were not injured. But the other three may want some medical attention for their headaches.

"The crate and its contents are inside, untouched, along with the three sailors and the fellow we believe was driving the truck. We didn't want to touch anything until you got here. I believe you should be the one to identify what we have. Right now, since the goods have not left the country, I am merely glad to have stopped a theft of our product from our plant." I paused to let this entire story sink in for Reiter.

"Really, Mr. Christian. Do you expect me to believe it is as simple as you say? Your team just managed to get onto the roof of a two-story building, get inside and subdue four armed men? We know who you may have detained here based on Rutger's briefing and the intelligence he has passed along. If we are right, and I will know shortly, we are dealing with a Russian gunrunning operation. I doubt your private investigators had the capability to manage this crew.

"Let's get inside." With that Reiter picked up his radio and summoned an entry squad.

"Captain, if I may. Please. Can we go in, just you and me? I would like you to survey the scene first. Then bring your crew in. It should take but a few minutes. The scene is secure."

Reiter hesitated, but seemed to realize the breach team wasn't necessary. He agreed and began walking with me. I took a quiet deep breath. I wanted Reiter to know that this could be a mess for us, and we were the good guys. I wanted him in the right frame of mind to put a good spin on what he was about to see, especially with a dead guy in the back.

The warehouse was not any better lit than when we entered, but the scene was recognizable. Basically, there was an empty truck, a large wooden crate on a pallet skid with our company paperwork still stapled to it. And four guys taped to the top and sides of the crate. Their guns were piled next to their unconscious forms.

"You do realize how improbable this seems, right?" He asked.

I merely shrugged my shoulders.

Reiter's eyes were adjusting to the dark as I introduced Peter, Kent and Tyler. I could tell right away Reiter recognized something in common with my team. His acknowledgement was simple, "Gentlemen." Then he shook their hands, "Well done."

My team acknowledged in kind. They just nodded.

Kent spoke, "Captain, there is the matter of the two outside. We should get the one inside before he freezes out there and see what he has to say."

"Before we go, Mr. Christian, I want my team in here now to secure the scene. Then we shall proceed to the back." Reiter called in his squad, advising them the scene was secure. He told them he wanted the evidence preserved and that there were four arrests

We walked outside toward the rear of the building. As we approached, he saw the vessel tied to the docks. "Russian," he said. "Look at the vessel numbers and the Cyrillic lettering. Very good."

He got on his radio and added another member to the squad inside. "He will be able to translate for us, if our arrested friends do not speak German."

As we turned the first corner, he asked "Who was the person from your team that discovered this?"

Tyler was about to answer, but I discourage him with a shake of my head.

"Let's take a look at the scene, Captain. I would value your opinion as to what really happened. Then we can have our man fill in the details as to him finding the men here like this. He has touched nothing."

Reiter must have suspected I was playing some kind of con. But he was veteran enough to realize this could go down several ways, so he chose to keep his options open. “That is fine.” He replied.

We turned the second corner where we came upon a pretty gruesome scene.

First Reiter took in the body. “Looks like a large caliber bullet. Lots of damage to the side of the face, but more at the back of the head. It looks like he was shot here, all this blood. His hands do not appear to be damaged, so we can check for fingerprints and other evidence when we get the body to the morgue.”

He shone a flashlight around in the gravel and found the Makarov. “Is this one of yours?” he asked pointing his light at the gun.

I replied, “We are not armed sir.”

He got to his radio and called two more of his team to join us. “They will secure this scene and the gun. Now where is the other one?”

Kent walked us over to the dumpster and pointed out the other guy, hands bound behind him and snoring heavily into a gag. A crusty scab had formed on the right side of his head from a blow. Reiter gave him several rough shakes until he awoke. The man moaned.

“What is your name?” Reiter asked him.

“Tobiaz, Tobiaz Addamski. Oh my God, my

head hurts."

"Who did this to you Addamski?" Reiter asked.

"Oh, my God! Am I shot? My head – am I shot?"

"Addamski, you are not shot. Now tell us what happened." Reiter insisted.

"Gennady was going to shoot me. In the face. That son of a bitch. Then his head exploded right in front of me. One minute he was looking at me with a mean grin. The next, his face blew up. I was still taking it all in, when my head felt like it had exploded too. Then everything went black. I guess I thought I had died. Wait! What about Anatoly? Is Anatoly dead too?"

"Who is Anatoly?" Reiter asked.

Tobiaz must have realized that he was in deep trouble babbling about Russians with the police hovering over him and him still being restrained. "I prefer not to say anything else right now until I talk with my lawyer. I need a doctor."

Just as it happens in the States, he had dummied up.

Reiter ordered two of his team to search the boat for identification and anything else they could find. Now that it was docked in Germany, he was confiscating it for investigative purposes. One of his men helped the still-bound Addamski to his feet and we all headed back inside.

Reiter pulled me aside as we walked. "Very neat package Mr. Christian. Four smugglers inside, at least three of whom are likely Russian, possibly even the fourth, given Addamski's reference to Anatoly. We have an unconscious Pole, and what appears, by the name Gennady, a dead Russian outside. How fortunate for you that none of your men are armed, yet none of your men are injured, especially given the proliferation of AK-47s, a dead man, and the Makarov out back. Yes, very fortunate, wouldn't you say?"

I was about to answer in the affirmative when he said, "Don't. Please don't say anything. I like the story exactly the way it seems. I do not want to complicate it with the truth."

Inside the warehouse Reiter's guys had cut Anatoly and the Russian seamen free and had handcuffed them. By the time we returned they had also fully pried off the wooden lid of the crate. On the floor in the warehouse, a police photographer was capturing an array of what seemed to be four or five dozen Kalashnikovs, several dozen Makarov pistols and several dozen cases of ammunition. There was cosmoline-soaked gun paper strewn in a pile alongside the crate.

"Captain," one of the officers said, pointing

to the display.

"Yes, Walter. I see. Make sure your photographs show these four standing by this cache. Capture everything and then see this is re-crated. Inventory it here before we leave and inventory it again as soon as you get to our command post. Ensure each item is photographed, tagged and marked for the federal prosecutor. And save the gun wrapping paper for fingerprints."

Reiter turned to us. "Gentlemen, on its face, this is a very good piece of police work. As a courtesy to you, Herr Felder and Polizeiobermeister Becker, have asked that you come into their station in the morning to give your statements. This must have been a long night for you."

I was about to remind Reiter that we were not acting in a police capacity, merely private investigators on an internal investigation, when I thought the better of it. This was when silence was truly golden. I thanked him, nodded to my crew and they joined me in leaving the building.

We were all pretty tired. It seemed like days since I had any sleep. Then I realized it *had* been days since I slept. It must have shown on my face because Tyler said, "You look like hell. Let's get you back to your hotel so you can grab a few hours sleep."

I had to admit, it sounded like a damned good idea.

As we headed back to Reinbeck, I called Rutger and gave him a full briefing, of our official version that is. I told him we would join him in the morning to give formal statements. He asked, “Mike, do you have any idea what time it is? It is already five-thirty. I am up, having coffee and will be in the office in less than an hour. You should be back in Reinbeck about seven forty-five. I will see you about nine o’clock.”

It really is true what they say, *No job is finished until the paperwork is done*. I also had to check in with my boss and update him. It had been a while and he hadn’t called. With something looming as expensive as this was, I wasn't sure if that was a vote of confidence or dismissal.

No sleep, not just yet.

Chapter Sixteen

THE CALL TO BRINTON WENT BETTER than I expected, even though it was only one a.m. in New Jersey. He was pleased on all counts. Especially on getting the plant up in one day. We would be at full production by the second day of my arrival and that was fine, given what he thought would take a week of legal battles. His savings, if they could be called that, could be ten million dollars. At least the losses in non-performance penalties were reduced by that much. I would leave it to him and his people to provide the proper media and customer relations spin.

He wasn't very happy about the fact that we came upon Russians moving arms within our plant operations, or the fact there was a dead-body aspect to the story. I could tell he didn't buy the official version, but he was too smart to ask any probing questions. He asked me to keep the Germans quiet on that Russian business. I told him I would check but held no hopes for that. It was completely out of our control. I would have to check with Felder and Becker. I wasn't even sure that my team or I were out of the woods yet and told him so. He assured me our attorneys would handle that mess if it arose but to be on the safe side, he would begin making those calls to start that process immediately.

He also asked me if I thought Warner knew who was involved with the smuggling in the plant and I replied that I didn't think so. I knew that wouldn't bode well for Warner either. If Warner had known and done nothing, it was bad for him. And if he hadn't known what was going on under his nose, that would not bode well for him either. He was as good as gone. On the other hand, he wasn't going to jail.

We talked about the various employees involved. His recall was impressive as he asked individually, by name, what should be done with each. He wasn't patronizing me. He wanted my input to his decision. He also asked me to ensure that Felder got any support he needed, no matter what course he chose relative to prosecuting our employees.

Brinton thanked me for a good job and

urged me to get home quickly, mumbling something about a problem with a new business venture in Moscow.

■ ■ ■ ■ ■

Tyler, Peter, Kent and I walked into Felder's office together. I had seen this type of display of power before in government settings. The flags of Germany, Hamburg and Berlin hung on polished wooden staffs behind his seven-foot wide mahogany desk. A matching wood rack of fountain pens held two beautiful Mont Blanc Meisterstücks. The glass top on the desk had not a speck of dust. The only paperwork on it was his case file of this investigation. On top of that was what appeared to be Reiter's hand-written report. Behind the desk, on the matching credenza, was a photograph of Felder with Chancellor Helmut Kohl. I was impressed, as was the intention.

Herr Jaeger Felder and Rutger Becker welcomed us curtly and formally. No coffee, no pastries.

Felder began, "Please be seated gentlemen. Captain Reiter has filed a full report. This is quite an interesting piece of investigative work. But Reiter's report, although a good story, leaves some questions to be answered. How would you say, some loose ends to clean up?

Wouldn't you agree?"

I was worried that if this turned into separate interrogations of my team and me, the final compilation would be ugly. But if I were running their case, that is exactly what I would do.

So, I quickly took ownership of the direction he wanted to go.

"Indeed, gentlemen. I agree that we need to ensure the facts align to your satisfaction. But before we begin, may I take a moment to say what a pleasure it has been to work with Herr Becker and your special response team. We were all very impressed. And we also want to ensure you that our corporate headquarters has already been made aware of the level of cooperation and energy your people have brought to bear on solving this complex case. Our chief executive himself asked me to convey to you his thanks and that of our entire workforce of fourteen hundred of your citizens, for returning the plant and for resolving this tragic abuse of our trust. He has also already spoken with the German Ambassador to the United States and expressed his satisfaction with the way you have resolved this. He praised both of you and Captain Reiter by name. I am also to assure you that you will receive complete support from our company—witnesses, documentation and access. Everything you need. As you can see, we want this investigation to be as clear, consistent and accurate as you do. Now, how may we help you?"

Jaeger looked at me for the longest while. Rutger just looked down and smiled to himself. He knew they had been placed in a satin lined box. There would be no separate questioning. Now it was a matter of how Felder wanted to back off that plan.

Jaeger made eye contact with Rutger and began. "Gentlemen. I must say I was not sure I was comfortable with having a private investigation take place on German soil. Regardless of your bona fides Michael, you simply waltzed in and took over while I was sidelined by my own management. Nor was I comfortable backing off my decision to close the plant. There was even a side of me that secretly needed you to fail. Otherwise, I would have been shown up by a private investigator."

At that point, I almost wanted to object to being called a private investigator. I was the head of security for one of the largest corporations in the world. But again, I hesitated just long enough for him to continue.

"However, you and your team have proven up to the task of helping us close this case. We are all very grateful. And Reiter's report generously shows that *we* solved the case with your help."

"We also know that there is very much more to this story than anyone cares to have formally documented. Those are the loose ends, Michael. So, it is here that I must ask you for the full cooperation you have promised."

I was hoping the tension I was beginning to feel wasn't showing on my face.

"Michael, if you could give us a statement of your observations, this will be adequate for our final report." Jaeger Felder did not become a senior prosecutor by being politically naïve. He knew the deck was already stacked in our favor and he surely wasn't going to buck the American or the German ambassador. He also did not want it on record that he made a deal with an American "cowboy" to run his own investigation, using hired gunslingers without close police supervision, even if Becker was embedded, perhaps more so *because* Becker was embedded.

I was very grateful we had this level of support and participation from the German government. At a lower level, the bureaucracy would not have allowed this latitude in decision-making. And having Brinton grease the skids at the highest levels didn't hurt either.

He continued with a clean, crisp summary. "If I understand the facts as Captain Reiter reported them, he came upon the scene, just after you and your men arrived. You met his team in the yard and escorted him into the warehouse where he found four suspects bound to a shipping crate inside. A fifth suspect was outside, but he was dead from a gunshot wound. Yet another man was found taped up and unconscious outside. It appeared there had been some kind of internal struggle among the smugglers. A search of the crate the men were fastened to revealed a cache of illegal weapons and ammunition. And a search of the truck parked inside, revealed a crate filled with contraband cigarettes and liquor, none of which had the required tax stamps. Does that align with your recollection of what they found?"

I was not sure how to answer his question. It was a pretty good recall of the story I gave Reiter. What I didn't know was whether or not Reiter had told Felder it seemed like a bunch of bull, or if Reiter was corroborating my story.

Felder interrupted my thoughts. "I know. It seemed implausible to me too. But in light of the excellent results I am willing to close the case and deal with the Russians separately. Is Reiter's report accurate?"

"Other than the fact that we were not there when they searched the truck and found the cigarettes, yes."

Felder hesitated. “Michael, let me ask you again, Captain Reiter’s crew found cigarettes and liquor in a crate in your company truck. The crate was tagged with your company shipping papers. Do you now recall witnessing their discovery?”

I could see where he was going. Once we were back in the states, or wherever Tyler and his guys would disappear to, he would have no witnesses, other than his own people, to link the cargo to the plant and to our inside people. He needed to prove that he and Becker had been on the right track, that the plant closing had been justified and that solving this case was a major coup on their part.

“Herr Felder, I was a witness to the fact that there were cigarettes and liquor in a crate with our company papers on them. Yes.”

“Very good, then. We will have a brief statement of these facts drawn up for your signature. I also respectfully request the original signed statements or confessions of Jürgen Jentzil, Altman Bauer and Tasha Krause-Boryenko. Then you can go.” With that, Felder called for his assistant and dictated something to her in German. He asked if we wished for some coffee, and I was only too eager for some caffeine. I was running on fumes.

Becker spoke up. “Tobiaz has learned that

his brother Karol has been murdered by Gennady, who admitted that just before he was killed. Tobiaz claims not to have killed Gennady. Our initial take on that is he is telling the truth. We will confirm that within the hour when his gunshot residue tests come back."

"We have no witnesses to that shooting, other than what Tobiaz reports. We have also learned from Tobiaz that he and Karol are related to a fellow who works at your plant. Although he is currently refusing to give up the name, he will identify who that person is. Tobiaz also does not know that Altman Bauer has already named his cousins Tadeusz and Ulrich. We are pressuring him to deal with us in exchange for dropping what he thinks is a charge for murdering Gennady. That will give us independent corroboration against your inside drivers. Your Tasha and Bauer account for the link to Pavel Oveshkin and the guns, the link to smuggling cigarettes and liquor, and to Bauer using his plant authority to provide the means for the guns to move to Rostock and Warnemunde and out of the country. Your customs paperwork will be positively linked as coming from your order entry system, but without company permission or awareness. So yes, we appreciate your cooperation."

Touché! He knew had me there and so he

continued his summary.

"We also have three Russians who have entered the country illegally and they will be criminally charged. Normally they would be merely deported. But we will hold them a while before we notify their embassy. Our relationship with the Russians is still a bit uncomfortable. Anyway, I believe we may be able to connect our prisoners and Anatoly with Tasha's Pavel Oveshkin. He's the guy Interpol thinks is linked to arms dealing for Sergey Miloradov of the Russian mafia in Moscow."

"At the moment, the Russians are not talking. But we will charge them with illegal entry, federal weapons transfers, possession of illegal and unauthorized automatic weapons, smuggling, murder, and conspiracy to commit murder. I am sure they will be willing to help us a bit."

Felder and Becker had a handle on the entire case and all the elements of its potential. I just wanted a quick jolt of robust German coffee and to sign my statement and go. Before the coffee arrived, Felder's assistant was back with a one-page document that simply stated what he needed to corroborate Reiter's telling of the events. I signed. My team and I walked out amid handshakes and promises to send them the confessions and to stay in touch. Kent and

Rutger hung back to talk a bit.

I had no energy left. If I had, I would have liked to stay another day or two, just to see more of Hamburg. But this was the same as all the other trips. Solve the problem and head back home. Perhaps I will return another day and bring Alice.

I asked if anyone needed a ride to the airport. Tyler and Peter declined. They had a car to return and the guys wanted to ride back together. No doubt to reminisce and bond. For all I knew, they were spending another night in town near the airport in Hamburg and hooking up with Rutger. We spoke in complimentary terms to each other and talked about how we enjoyed the experience.

No one mentioned the collateral damage behind the warehouse. It was as if it had never happened. This was certainly not their first exposure to the secrets of necessity. This is the kind of experience that bonds soldiers or law enforcement officers. I promised that I would call Morgan and thank him for his excellent choices and compliment the outstanding work they did. They seemed to shrug that off as if to say it wasn't necessary. I would be sure to include ample bonus money for them in my payment to Morgan.

Friedrich was waiting in a no standing zone

for me. As he saw me shake hands with the guys, he pulled up. “Friedrich, take me to the office. I have some papers I need to gather for you to deliver to prosecutor Felder. Then I want you to take me to the hotel and wait for me. I am checking out and heading directly to the airport.”

My non-stop flight home would take over eleven hours. I had booked the last remaining first-class ticket. Exhaustion was taking over and I could not wait to get home. When I got to the hotel, I called my wife. The call rolled over to voicemail, so I left her a long rambling message about being okay, heading home, eleven-hour flight and two more hours from the New Jersey airport, “I love you. I miss you.” All the things you say at the end of an engagement when you are completely wrung out and finally going home. I knew I should bring her a souvenir of the trip, but I would get that at the airport.

As Friedrich drove me from the hotel to the airport, it occurred to me that I had been awake since I left Detroit almost three days ago. I was weak and dizzy. I decided that when I got on the plane, I’d have a nice glass of Crown Royal to celebrate my victory. and to help me get some sleep on the flight home. I would get a nice long rest crossing back over the Atlantic. No Concorde for me on the return trip.

▪ ▪ ▪ ▪ ▪

As I settled into my seat, the flight attendant brought me a dark golden drink poured over ice. I sipped and let the warm soothing elixir calm me. I slid the window shade closed, leaned back in my seat, shut my eyes and reexamined the events of the last seventy hours.

I had flashbacks to my childhood, of hiding under my desk in school during "air raid" drills. We were taught that we had a chance of surviving Russian nuclear attacks if we rolled up in little balls and covered our heads like tiny kittens. I remembered the nuclear missile crisis of the 1960s when we knew we would die the next day if Khrushchev launched missiles down on us from Cuba. And I thought of my surprise when I got here to find the feared Russians were somehow involved in a smuggling operation. I basked in the self-satisfaction of surviving threats, imagined and real, at the hands of the Russians. I reveled in the glow of Brinton's brief praise for "fixing" the problem and for getting his plant back. It was more than many got from him. My hungry ego was satisfied for now.

I smiled and mused to myself, as I had so many times before, I love my job. It almost seems like fiction. Maybe someday I should write a book before it's too late.

About the Author

MIKE SAAD IS A FORMER SECURITY executive for several of the largest corporations in the world. For the last forty years he has traveled extensively investigating and "fixing" corporate problems, much like Michael Christian does.

To further treat you, Mike draws on his experiences from over ten years as a decorated officer on the Detroit Police Department, in their Tactical Mobile Unit and in the secret and elite Wayne County Organized Crime Task Force, where he led complex investigations into mafia activities and into international theft and fencing cases.

Mike has spent a lifetime mentoring, teaching and supporting professional security practices in his field. Now he turns those experiences from education to entertainment.

He has been awarded the *Lifetime Designation of Certified Protection Professional* by ASIS International, the premier professional security organization in the world, who has also designated him a *Life Member*.

Mike is retired and lives in Michigan with his wife of thirty-five years.

Sneak Peek at the next Michael Christian Mystery

TURN THE PAGE FOR A PREVIEW OF Michael Christian's next investigation. Moscow is the setting where Christian must face Pavel Oveshkin, this time in league with the Russian Mafia.

MICHAEL CHRISTIAN, travels to Moscow, when his company gets crossways with the Russian Mafia. He has to determine if the plant manager is making illegal payments or if he is being extorted. Regardless, Christian must fix it.

His mission is complicated when the CIA asks him to keep an eye out for some missing items. Namely dirty bombs built by the KGB. A handful have gone missing and both governments are trying to find them before they end up in terrorist hands. Any extra eyes can help, including Christian's and those of his contacts abroad.

Christian has to rely on a former KGB agent for help with the mafia. The FBI legal attaché and the Agency seem to have abandoned Christian when Pavel Oveshkin re-emerges as a possible candidate for the stolen bombs. When he needs their help the most, he is on his own.

A Dollar Short

A Michael Christian Mystery

Mike Saad

Moscow, Russia

IT ALL HAPPENED SO FAST AND professionally. *Just like in the movies*, he thought. Carter had deftly slipped his new Mercedes Benz E500 into his marked parking space at the office, his name freshly lettered on the curb – *Winston*. As he turned off the big engine he smiled to himself, thinking about his position in life. He was a senior director of one of the largest multi-national corporations in the world, running a foreign start-up in Russia, immediately after the dissolution of the Soviet Union. In his mind's eye, he could clearly see where he was on the fast track to his next promotion and a significant pay increase, another one.

His car still smelled new and the leather creaked richly as he stepped out and bent over to retrieve his briefcase off the rear seat. The moment he straightened up, he was forcefully shoved back in the car and hammered by something hard in the back of his right ear. His vision exploded into red and white stars and he felt an electric jolt run down through his shoulders as his cervical spine compressed onto its discs. Then he passed out. When he awoke he was here, in what seemed to be a warehouse.

▪ ▪ ▪ ▪ ▪

Carter had no idea how much time had passed while he was unconscious. When he tried to lift himself off the floor, every movement sent excruciating pain through his head. He threw up the first time he tried to stand. He figured he had a concussion and was terrified he would die without proper medical attention. He tried to inventory himself for other injuries. He was unable to move his hands, which seemed bound tightly behind his back. His fingertips felt swollen and cold. His feet were bound with tape at the ankles.

Each time he tried to open his eyes, even the low ambient light in the room sent bolts of pain through his eyes to the front of his head. He was dizzy to the point of passing out. His collar was stiff and had a sweet metallic smell that he recognized as his own blood, probably from where he had been struck. He tried to lie perfectly still since the slightest movement caused intense pain. He began to feel the cold of the floor and realized he was lying on rough, unsealed concrete. He began shivering as his now alert body recognized the chill. He knew he was a prisoner. No one had to tell him he had been kidnapped.

Carter had imagined scenarios all his life where he would be called on to be brave. The first was when he was a boy, confronted by the school bully and told to give up his lunch money. All the kids were watching, and no one would help him. He was on his own. In his fantasy, he would talk the bigger kid out of hurting him. He could see himself using logic and reason to explain why he should be left alone. In Carter's moment of bravery, the befuddled oaf would laugh at him, give him a small shove and walk away, leaving Carter broke, but unharmed.

As a fan of his high school teams, he would stand in the bleachers and watch the athletes bang it out on the field. In his fantasy, Carter would be lined up against the biggest, meanest kid on the defensive line. Just before the ball was snapped, Carter would whisper into his opponent's helmeted facemask, "just fall down when I hit you and it won't hurt as much." To his deep satisfaction, the larger and meaner football player would take a dive when he was hit, creating a hole large enough for the halfback to run through and score the winning touchdown. His teammates would cheer his well-delivered block, bravely rendered against all odds.

As a young man sitting in his cubicle at work, Carter would imagine the scenario where the office manager would assign him the hardest work and take all the credit. At the leadership meeting Carter would look his manager daringly in the eye, then stand to tell the department head that the report he was reviewing was based on Carter's work and not that of his manager. The department director would admire Carter's boldness as well as his creative work product. Of course, Carter would get the promotion (and the girl) and live happily ever after.

Truth be told, Carter was not that brave of a guy. But he was quite intelligent and not afraid of hard work. He was determined to get ahead, advancing rapidly. In time, he became the department director. He spun failing operations into efficient, profitable entities. He was recognized as skilled in turning around sluggish processes, saving tons of money in re-investment costs or plant closings. He then helped his company's business start-ups in emerging markets. He was doing exactly that in Moscow, in post-Soviet Union Russia. Now he wished he had all the bravery of his fantasies.

When he was transferred to Russia, the company Security executive had someone brief him about situations like this. He was told that corporate kidnappings had become commonplace throughout Russian metropolitan areas and Moscow in particular. He had been given the background on the power of the Russian Mafia and the fact that they were regularly kidnapping western businessmen and extorting their companies or their families. The security expert had told him that he must be vigilant, keep a low profile, build a security plan, avoid the train stations, don't hire taxis off the curb. Carter thought he was exaggerating. He pegged the guy as one who had no real role in performing business risk analysis, someone who was frightening him just to make himself look important.

The lawyers and finance guys had already done their risk assessments. Carter believed the company would not knowingly send him to a place that was really as dangerous as the security guy said. There was also something else about the security briefing that was causing Carter to feel sick to his stomach now. He was told the United States government had an official and immutable policy that they don't pay ransoms and they won't allow ransom demands to be paid to foreign kidnappers. He had also been told that the FBI had no official role in Russia if something like this should happen to a U.S. businessman.

So, when they came for him in his cell the first time, he concluded his best opportunity was to be brave and rational. Carter thought himself a very smart man. He decided he would logically explain that ransom attempts would be futile. He told them the U.S. government would not pay and his company could not pay. He explained to them that the best solution would be to blindfold and return him to his workplace – no harm, no foul. He never finished his explanation.

His captors laughed at him, then they beat him with a rolled-up newspaper. After only three solid punches to the face, he passed out from the pain in his head. He awoke lying in his own vomit.

So, rather than calling his office to make a kidnap demand, they forced him to give them his home phone number in the States. That call to his wife ended horribly. Now he was on the floor of the warehouse again. Carter was bleeding, broken and feared desperately for his life. He would have to figure something else out to avoid further beatings and to get out of here alive. Wherever "here" was.

The call to his wife went the opposite of

what Carter had expected. Once Carol realized he had been taken, she sounded terrified and unintelligible in the phone. Her hysteric words ran together and her sobs drowned out her answers. They had been married for eight years, yet he could barely make out what she was trying to say. The Russians had a harder time. They became angry and frustrated and hung up on her without even being sure she understood their instructions for the ransom payment. They were however able to warn her not to notify the police or the FBI. They couldn't take out their exasperation on his wife, so they hung up on her. They took it out on Carter.

They started with their bare fists, knocking out a tooth. The swelling of his cut lips was so painful he couldn't form his own words. His head throbbed so loudly he thought it would explode. He vomited again and passed out in the first few minutes. They doused him with water and woke him. They taunted him in Russian while they beat him again—this time on his ribs with a telephone book. Carter thought he would die of suffocation. The pain from trying to breathe was so horrible that he figured he had a couple broken ribs. Each breath stabbed in his chest.

Then they tied him upright to the chair, so he could breathe. His eyes had swollen shut after only a few punches. He could hear his captors but not see them. He didn't know if they wanted anything at all anymore. They seemed happy merely to be beating him. He was terrified, unable to muster up any of the imagined courage he was so good at as a young man. His spirit had broken in a matter of hours. Carter realized he would never be able to talk or fight his way out of this. He was now worried that he might be killed even should they pay the ransom.

He awoke back in his cell with no idea how long he had been sleeping or unconscious. He could hear them coming for him again in his cell. They were big, strong men who physically over powered him each time. This time they tied him, straddling and facing the back of that damn chair again. He had lost count of the days. One, two, three? His room had no windows, making it difficult to tell. One of his captors spoke in heavily accented English, "Why do they not pay? Is your miserable life worth nothing to wife? What about wife? Why she no make payment?" He punctuated each question by slashing a narrow leather belt across Carter's back, which was becoming a mass of bleeding welts. He squirmed in his chair and began crying, even before the next swoosh whipped through the air.

Essex, New Jersey, USA

MICHAEL CHRISTIAN WALKED CASUALLY down the corridor that joined the company fitness center to the corporate wing. His office there took up the northwest corner of the ground floor. The hedonistic side of him reveled in the spacious paneled room with its tall walls and drape-covered, floor-to-ceiling windows. The glass was coated with a metal reflectorized glaze that looked mirrored from the outside. In reality, the thin barrier formed an acoustically protective screen that prevented electronic eavesdropping from the outside. But Christian spent very little time in his office. Mostly it was used for entertaining visitors, either security contractors or government investigators of one sort or another.

Christian spent most of his time on airplanes for destinations in the US or in foreign countries. As the global head of security for a Fortune 50 company with three divisions, travel had become a regular part of his routine and a growing part of his job duties. He was the corporate "problem solver". And the problems always involved some type of ethics violation or criminal malfeasance committed by employees, or against them or the company. He was constantly on the go. It was starting to wear on his home life and the stress was mounting. He was as equally involved in responding to crises occurring in real time as he was in responding to issues that had already occurred. In any case, his job was to *fix things.*

As word of his successes got out, more of the company's managers discovered his talents and his discretion. They increasingly called on him to help solve their security "troubles". He had a small staff of experts and a raft of outside consultants fully capable of helping him and they too were always busy. Depending on the problem, he could beckon a surveillance crew, a handwriting analyst, or a data forensic investigator. And he could manage multiple issues simultaneously with those resources. That didn't slow the requests from group presidents around the world though. They wanted him to be on site personally to provide the same results he brought to other seemingly "insurmountable" problems.

It wasn't that his company was ethically void. It was just that with over one hundred thousand employees there were bound to be some bad apples. His company, Transeget Industries, also did business in some places conducive to criminal behavior. Then there was the one-off espionage case that came up nearly every month as a competitor or foreign government tried to gain unauthorized access to TI secrets. There was a lot on his security department plate and the piles kept growing.

His good friend and the company's chief medical officer, Al Korker, had prescribed regular exercise to relieve the stress and to build up Christian's resistance to physical and psychological fatigue. So a year ago he joined the company fitness program and was working out daily with a cardiac fitness coach in the executive gym. He was also working out on alternate dates with a strength conditioning and a Tae Kwan Do coach. Christian had rebuilt his rough form from years ago. In his late thirties, he was as fit as when he was a cop in his twenties. He smiled in satisfaction. He was fit. He felt it and looked it. And working out at 5:30 each morning seemed to fit his lifestyle just fine.

"Michael, Mike!" A voice called out to him from behind. He recognized it without turning around.

He stopped. “Hi Marianne, what’s up?” Marianne Callucci was the executive administrative assistant to the Chief Executive Officer of Transeget Industries. There were executive vice presidents making ten times her salary, but none was more powerful than she. The fact that Marianne was walking the halls looking for Christian before 7:00 in the morning alerted him that something was in the works.

“Barry wants to see you right away, in his private office.” It didn’t surprise Christian that his boss was already at work. He was over 60 years old, seemed to work 24 hours a day and never looked tired. Barry Brinton was one of the most respected businessmen in the world. He had singlehandedly taken this twenty-six-billion-dollar company and turned it from a marginal performer to a winner. Their stock price soared.

His group presidents lived in a mixture of loyalty, fear and awe of him. He was a corporate ass-kicker and a Wall Street favorite. When Barry Brinton talked, investors around the world listened for clues about where to place their money or when to remove it. He had singlehandedly and forcefully managed a stock-split and brought TI’s price back up to its original position in one year.

Brinton had no time for small talk and usually had minions to handle just about anything that came up. Asking Christian to join him in his private office left him a bit unsettled. Brinton had another, more public office where he met with just about everyone.

True to his status as a corporate magnate, that office was tastefully decorated to establish his role as an executive who ranked in the top layer of his peers around the world. But his most private conversations were in an office that Christian had personally secured. He had also personally overseen the soundproofing of the room at the level of *Sensitive Compartmented Information Facility* according to US government standards. A *SCIF,* as it was called, was rarely seen at corporate executive levels. Although Brinton was big on corporate privacy, a *SCIF* was a significant investment and went a bit farther than one had to go to protect private company information. TI was publicly known as a long-time government contractor and often participated voluntarily in "special projects" or "requests for assistance" as some agencies referred to them.

"Private office Marianne? Can you give me a clue as to what I am walking into?" He asked.

"Sorry, Mike. He just said to find you and get you there immediately. I guess I can tell you that he's not alone though." She turned and began walking back to the executive wing.

Although she did not have Christian by the elbow, she might just as well have grabbed him. She was very self-confident and had earned the right to be. Christian liked working with her. She was the ultimate professional and totally committed to her boss. But she favored Christian with tidbits of information to make his life a bit easier with Brinton. Trusting that level of confidence, Christian pressed on as they walked.

"Who's there Marianne? Anybody I should be aware of?"

"I think you may know at least one of them Mike, but they are not *ours*." Christian knew she meant they were outsiders. Neither board members, nor corporate executives. The suspense of a meeting with outsiders in Brinton's secure office was intoxicating to him. This was the kind of thing that made his job so exciting. He couldn't wait to get to the meeting.

As they got on the private elevator to TI's top floor he asked, "Do you think you could have someone rustle up a bite for me to eat? I'm famished and was on my way to the dining room when you caught me." Christian was very careful not to presume that Marianne's job description included schlepping coffee for anyone, including Brinton.

"I've already had someone see to that.

There should be a warm breakfast for you all when you get there." She replied. Christian felt a bit foolish. He should have known. Marianne would have already anticipated and provided for that, just like she managed all Brinton's business and social calendar requirements. It didn't matter who you were, you couldn't get to see the boss without approval from Marianne.

The elevator quietly opened and Bill Jennings, the security officer, nodded to them. The plain clothed executive protection agent had seen them approach on the security monitor for the camera in the executive elevator. Jennings was a former US Secret Service agent that Christian had hired from active service. Jennings had been in the field, serving on a protection detail for a former vice president and was an alternate instructor on advanced executive protection techniques at the Service's academy in Georgia. A friend of Christian's in the FBI had recommended Jennings based on personal experiences when the two agencies actually played nice together.

"Mr. Christian. Good to see you sir. Mr. Brinton is waiting for you and asked that you go right in." He swiped an electronic ID card in front of the sensor, pressed his personal five-digit code into the touchpad and opened the door to Brinton's office. He stepped part way inside and quietly stated, “Mr. Christian is here sir,” and then he stepped aside. Christian entered and the door closed behind him with a solid but quiet thud and the snap of a heavy-duty lock. A secure electronic deadbolt imbedded two and a half inches into a steel frame and a magnet, capable of withstanding 900 pounds of force, sealed the door shut along the top doorframe.

The space also served as Brinton’s safe-hiding room. It wasn’t a secret space but with other security embellishments, it was virtually penetration proof. There was independent backup power, separate telecommunications, a satellite phone always charging and food and drink for a week. It was a mini war room and it suited Brinton’s style just fine.

Brinton’s private office was neatly, but not spartanly outfitted. A Telluride executive desk with a leather writing-surface sat off to the left side of the room in front of a matching cabinet-front hutch. Paired lateral files and credenzas neatly lined the walls under Old English country-side lithographs. An out-of-context, personally cast, Remington bronze of “Coming Through the Rye” sat on one of them. A news reporter had once called him a cowboy, referring to Brinton’s rough and ready style. Marianne arranged for the bronze horseback-riding cowboys to be in his office the following week. She pulled that off in spite of the advertised requirement for a five-thousand-dollar deposit and a projected timeline of four to five weeks for a private casting. No one but Marianne knew the final price tag on the work of art.

There was a small conference table in the room and more casual seating on several leather armchairs and a small love seat. Persian rugs covered the black mahogany floors and not a board squeaked when Christian crossed the room to greet his boss.

"Mr. Brinton." Christian greeted his CEO formally, out of respect while in the presence of others. Brinton replied, "You can dispense with the formalities Mike. I believe you know Cam Cross."

Cameron Cross was with the Central Intelligence Agency and was a corporate liaison officer. TI was his "account". They had met on several occasions when Christian was briefed into certain events. He doubted that Cross was the government official's real name. The agent rose from his seat, walked across the room and extended his hand. "Good to see you again Michael. I'd like you to meet an associate of mine, William Walters." It was all Christian could do to keep from chuckling out loud. *William Walters.* Whether that was his real name or not, it seemed too hokey to be real. Christian nodded, "Walters."

Brinton started right in. "Please sit. Help yourself to some coffee or breakfast while we get you up to speed."

Christian stood at the breakfast bar laid out on a credenza at the back wall and poured himself a cup of robust smelling black coffee. He opted away from the fruit, muffins and cereal for now. He had been read into a few programs already and all of the briefings were a bit intense. Having a stranger in the room led him to believe it was about to happen again. He didn't want to be distracted by eating. Walters began.

"It's not necessary to remind you, but I will do so anyway, Mr. Christian. You are still sworn to secrecy under the National Security Act, the Espionage Act and CNWDI. There is no end to the term of your oath of secrecy unless we specifically and in writing advise you accordingly." He then made a notation into a notebook he was carrying, as if checking off an obligation he had fulfilled.

"Wait a minute." Christian interrupted. "The Critical Nuclear Weapons Design Information level applies to this conversation?" Christian was playing a little bit dumb because he wanted clarification before allowing Walters to just blow through the secrecy requirements. He already knew that TI was involved in the US Government's Plowshares initiative with Russia.

Basically, the US would buy Russian weapons-grade uranium to reduce their arsenal. TI and others would then convert it into energy grade uranium and sell it back to Russia and other countries. They in turn would use it in their nuclear energy programs. The fact that a couple CIA agents were here talking about it was interesting, but a bit unsettling, especially given that he was being pulled into the conversation.

Walters continued, "We will keep this at a high-level Mr. Christian. For the moment we do not have an assignment that includes you specifically. But we may need your insight or the benefits of your observations on an upcoming trip. You are aware of the Plowshares program I presume."

Christian nodded but said nothing. He guessed their conversation was being covertly recorded by one or both of the agents.

"The program has hit a few snags and you may be aware of some of them. A few have even made world news. The Russians are playing fast and loose with us. The NATO contract calls for a fixed purchase price from the Russians. In turn the contract prescribes a fixed sell-back price. There is a little room for profit, with a small margin of error for delays, process break-downs and the like. But the margins are slim."

Christian glanced over at Brinton who raised his eyebrows as if to say *profits are not as good as I would like.* Walters proceeded, "Recently two things have happened that put the program more at risk. One is simply a matter of economics and was predictable. The Russians have raised the selling price to the Plowshares companies and have demanded lower buy-back prices. We do not know if they are serious about the pricing as a long-term rule or if they are using it as negotiating power for some other issue altogether."

"Regardless, the private corporations servicing the program, including yours, are being squeezed at both ends and the program is at risk. Obviously, so is national security if the Russian nuclear arsenal is not depleted under this initiative. We continue to draw down our arsenal according to our responsibilities, but the Russians are now behind schedule. Unfortunately, I can also assure you that neither our government energy agencies, nor the participants of the accord, are willing to subsidize your company for losses, even if that was a workable solution."

Christian saw this as a matter of bad business decision-making. Whether it was made to look like patriotism or not, it was either corporate greed or corporate profit taking that got TI involved. There also had to be a secret assumption that the government had too much at stake to let the private partner companies go bust over the deal. They were in it because there was presumably a buck to be made and for no other reason.

And now, predictably, the deal was going sour. Dealing with the Russians was always risky as was dealing with the Agency. The Russians didn't even understand or respect the word *partnership*. On the other hand, TI had made other global business decisions that caused Brinton to shut down operations when profitability went too far south. Christian knew his boss wouldn't hesitate to do so now if he felt it appropriate. Christian also had done this enough times to know he was not there to solve a profitability problem. Brinton must have already indicated he was willing to explore other solutions. He looked at Walters and said, "You want to tell him the *other* reason the program is in jeopardy, or should I?"

"Walters looked from Brinton to Cross to Christian, then continued, "Without going into specific inventory numbers, suffice it to say we have a very accurate count of the number of warheads and other materials that should have been brought into the program. The Russian nuclear commissioner and international inspectors have identified specific components to be decommissioned and their nuclear payloads re-purposed. From their launch sites around the Former Soviet Union Countries, missiles are shipped to and then disassembled at only three points in Russia. The warheads are removed, the payload securely repackaged and crated for shipment to the States. The entire process is under intense international monitoring during disassembly, containerization and transport."

"Similarly, less known, but of equal concern are the *suitcase* bombs. These are also nuclear weapons and there are about 40 of them covered in our agreement. We have been reprocessing them in accord with a sub-rosa clause in the covenant. This one is specifically between the Russian government and the US."

Christian looked at Brinton. He thought he was privy to most of the government contract terms, especially where there was a high-risk security requirement. Brinton looked away as if to say, *this is not the time or place for me to explain to you why you weren't included.*

Walters went on, "But when those shipments arrive at our reprocessing plants, the inventory count is short. Initially the Russians denied that they are shorting the sale and they refused to acknowledge the next obvious conclusion."

"And what's that?" Christian asked.

Walters looked at Cross then continued, "Somewhere out there, weapons grade uranium is floating around unaccounted for in the form of nuclear suitcase bombs." He seemed to pause for effect but needn't have bothered. The silence in the room grew deeper and if it was possible, the air seemed to become heavier. Almost imperceptibly, Brinton stirred in his seat. Christian thought he should be relieved to know that nuclear missiles weren't missing. But the idea that someone could carry a nuclear bomb in a suitcase was deeply disturbing. The fact they were dealing with the Russians made it even more so.

Walters continued, "As you can imagine, the US needs to make the world aware the program is at risk, but we cannot be talking in public about missing nuclear weapons. We need to do all we can to find out where those suitcases are and bring them back into the program. An added bonus would be to interdict those persons involved as well."

When it came to the agency, "interdicting someone" could mean anything at all. Christian thought he could see where this was going and didn't like it one bit. "And what does this have to do with us, other than our profits are being reduced? This seems an intelligence community problem or diplomatic or military issue. And if I may be so blunt, what does this have to do with me? Why am I being read into this level of the program?" He looked over at Brinton who was deliberately not returning his glance. Walters and Cross were also looking at Brinton who stood and went to the coffee setup and poured himself a cup. He spoke quietly.

"I will be sending you over to Moscow shortly Mike. We have another problem that was just brought to my attention, a serious internal issue. While there, you will likely use your access to Russian resources, entirely off the record, to help you solve that problem. I am guessing these will be people you trust and have worked with in the past. We have more than our Plowshares operations at risk here. Some of our people have gotten involved with the Russian mafia, it seems."

And Walters took over from there. "And while you are solving that problem, we would like you to use your relationships and their resources and see if you can learn what is going on with the missile program. You may get only rumor, hearsay, innuendo, denial or even false leads. But we need everything you can get. In fact, some of the rumors may have their basis in fact."

"We have our own resources pulling in and analyzing every lead and contact they have, but we also want to use less obvious avenues. We want to include every civilian resource at our disposal. And that is where you come in. We will leave the information gathering methods up to you. You will not be working for us. This is strictly a back-channel initiative, more of an informal request for assistance. You will be working as an employee of TI solving an internal issue. But we need you to dig as far as you can without exposing your involvement with us. Make it purely a financial-loss issue. Certainly, this is a business-based investigation you will be conducting. But if you happen to run across any information of value, and if you think you can share it, we would appreciate it."

"And Mr. Christian, as you would expect, the US government will deny this conversation ever took place. We will deny you work in conjunction with us. And if something should go wrong, you are entirely on your own and can expect no support from our agency or the United States government."

Christian believed him. Not only was there no sound leaving this room. There was no recorded evidence of the conversation ever taking place, except in the hands of the Agency itself. And he was sure Jennings would never say a word about who came to visit Brinton, if he even knew.

Christian looked again at Brinton who this time was looking him straight in the eye.

The silver-haired CEO looked almost grandfatherly as he said, "Mike, you can certainly say *No*. You can go over, solve our other problem, come straight home and there will be no corporate repercussions. Of course, we stand to lose millions here, if we cannot get the program on track or establish a business case for extracting ourselves from Plowshares. I would be grateful if you could help with that any way you and your people can. But the call is yours."

Brinton had just put himself on record in front of the Agency guys. He as much as said, *you don't have to do this*. And at the same time, he made it solely Christian's decision if he chose to go ahead with it. He had deftly established complete deniability if the shit hit the fan. Christian was screwed and he knew it. Everyone in the room knew it. But this was the price he paid for playing the game at this level. It was why they paid him the big bucks.

A DOLLAR SHORT … coming February 2019

Made in the USA
Monee, IL
11 August 2021

75478116R00194